Trouble Hunter

Trouble Hunter

A Western Story

Fred Grove

Five Star • Waterville, Maine

First Edition
Second Printing:

Published in 2006 in conjunction with Golden West Literary Agency.

Set in 11 pt. Plantin.

Printed in the United States on permanent paper.

Library of Congress Cataloging-in-Publication Data

Grove, Fred.
    Trouble hunter : a western story / by Fred Grove.—1st ed.
      p. cm.
    ISBN 1-59414-393-5 (hc : alk. paper)
    I. Title.
PS3557.R7T76 2006
813'.54—dc22   2006013250

Trouble Hunter

Chapter One

The trail to Red Cloud stretching out before Walt Durand near midday lay like a thin, dusty ribbon that beckoned across the prairie and wound lazily up to the sloping hills beyond. Although not a broad track, it was well defined, countless hoofs having churned into the soft earth, beaten down the blue stem grass, and pounded it into a hard-packed course.

And to Walt Durand, the manhunter, there was a feeling of comfort and security about the trail which he found pleasant, for he could scan the rolling swells on all sides and be certain of what lay around him. It gave him time to savor the country, and, manhunter or cowman, it made a rider envision great herds moving to market from the Indian Territory grasslands. His had been the one-man trail, the solitary camp, but here that was all distant, something to be put aside for a time. The open country was a relief to him after crossing the sand-tricky Arkansas where it bent southeast in its meandering division of the Osage and Pawnee nations. There, in the wooded bottomlands, he had first noticed a rider moving out ahead of him hurriedly. He sighted the man once more before he reached the flattening uplands, but had gradually dismissed him from his mind. A solitary horseman, moving in a hurry, was not unusual in the Territory.

Ahead of Durand now, arrow-straight to the northwest, curved the wandering course of a creek, and, beyond that, humped hills that squatted low and broad above the grass-rich flat lands like wary sentinels. Riding leisurely, he came to the tree-shadowed creek, pausing at the shallow, rocky ford to water his horse and roll a smoke. Here, out of the copper sun, the coolness of the trees and water smote him gently. As his horse heaved and raised its head, Durand mechanically inspected the opposite bank where the trail slanted up into a little valley before striding deeper into the hills. Many tracks had cut into the moist, dark footing, which was to be expected on a main trail, even to a small border bastion like Red Cloud. Yet the tracks were fresh and he had seen no one down the trail. It looked as if the riders had come from the valley to the creek, then turned back. To him tracks were like sign posts to the city traveler and he read them avidly, with a deep concentration and visualization. No shoeless Indian ponies' prints these; well shod cowmen's mounts had traveled this way.

So Durand left the creek's coolness and rode into the valley footing the hills, the question of the tracks not pressing, his thoughts concerned with Red Cloud and what might be there. Thus, when the first shot rang across the valley, he was in the open, an inviting target, and far from shelter. That blast, coming from the rim of the rocky ridge above him, staggered his horse as if the big dun-colored animal had been struck by the wild swing of a giant hand; a second shot sent the dun crashing down. Another bullet *thudded* into dying horseflesh before Durand could jerk free the short-barreled carbine. With the *crack* of high-powered rifles in his ears, he crouched behind the shuddering animal, hunting for a target in the glare of the sun.

After his horse went down, there was a short gap of silence; a restless, dangerous quiet it was, because the limestone ridge soon became alive with the steady *crack* of rifles from hidden gunmen. Durand detected no movement, and fierce anger, nettled by frustration at the lack of targets, ran through him like a fanned flame. It occurred to him that the well-concealed ambushers must have waited long for him and made sure of their positions. They had known he would pass through the valley. Now little geysers of dirt and loose rock sprang up near him like quick-groping mushrooms. He moved closer against the horse, virtually pinned there by the hail of lead. The safety of the tree-lined creek lay a good 200 yards behind him and nearby rocks offered less protection than the carcass of the horse. Sweat coursed down his body, and the carbine felt wet and slippery in his hands. Once, as he glanced up into the sun, a figure moved fleetingly behind a boulder high on the ridge. Durand snapped a shot and the Winchester bucked against his shoulder. An answering yelp of pain followed faintly and, for a moment, the hills and the little scooped-out valley were locked in silence. This was an unexpected turn for the riflemen—Durand was to be the marked meat of this bushwhacking trap. And to the sweating, tense man behind the dead horse, that cry of pain meant grim satisfaction as he swept the rocky slopes for another shot. *Damn them,* he thought, *they're playing it safe.* It was impossible to spot a man unless he moved. Seeing nothing, he settled down, depressing his long body as best he could and waiting for more bullets, and they came, not in spasmodic bursts, but steadily searching him out, probing for him. Sweat ran down his chest in rivulets. Smoke, pushed by a faint wind, drifted slowly across the valley, the wisps reminding him of buzzards he had seen hovering in a burning sky over dead horse or man.

So he lay there, sniping back when he could, wondering how long he could hold out, and waiting for night, when he figured he would hazard a desperate run for the creek behind him if his luck stayed stout and he didn't stop any lead. Scarcely any movement he made brought down a swarm of bumblebee sounds upon him, and he could hear the *thunk-thunk* of high velocity lead smashing into the barrier shielding him. The day wore on with half-step slowness. He thought it odd that his ambushers had made no attempt to outflank his position or get in behind him, but, when he looked at the uncovered slopes tapering toward the creek, he understood. Riding into this, high and open on a horse, he was supposed to have been dead by now, anyway. At first he had cursed the loss of a good horse; now he realized that its lifeless bulk and the scattered heap of rock rubble in which he lay were his salvation. From now until dark, it would be a game of waiting—and luck.

He figured he had ridden into the valley about noon. Now the sun, a great red furnace in the limitless, molten sky, showed mid-afternoon or later. This drygulching game puzzled him, the longer he thought about it, because there was no rhyme or reason to it so far as he could see. Larry Cramer was the only man he knew in Red Cloud and he was a stranger in this part of the country. Wryly he speculated if this could be a case of shooting at the wrong man. Or was it simply a trail killing and he happened to be the first unlucky rider who came along? Whatever it was, they had him cornered like a coyote run into a dead-end cañon. As best he could determine, at least three gunmen were blasting at him up there from the rock ledges and brush, and several times he thought he heard a fourth gun. On second thought, that many rifles seemed out of proportion for an ordinary hold-up or killing.

Durand peered again at the deadly ridge. His stirring brought an immediate response as lead slammed into the horse, knocked splinters from rocks, and sang past him. This was the game—a quick look for a shot, then duck and wait for the hail of lead that never failed to come like angry wasps. After that he gave up trying to unravel this, and lay motionless, cramped and sweating and sore-muscled, for a long time before risking another shot, merely watching. His shells were running low and he would need them tonight when he made his running fight afoot. He discovered presently, however, that conservation was impossible unless he allowed the rifleman on his left to move in closer. The killer had thrown two close slugs in succession at Durand's position, one bullet spitting dust into his face close to the ground. And Durand saw grimly that, unless that rifle was silenced or driven back from his flank, there would be no chance awaiting him after dark and he would go down like a trapped animal, helpless and unable to fight back. Abruptly, then, he rolled over, his carbine barked, and he fell back, awaiting a stormy answer from the ridge. It never came; the valley was wrapped in silence. For the first time he had shown himself and failed to draw fire. He could not understand this change in tactics, and he lay there, sweating, trying to read its meaning. It looked like a trap, a move to lure him out into the open and away from the horse. He grinned thinly—*Why, this was one of the oldest tricks in the game.*—and he decided to wait it out.

And then behind him suddenly sounded hoofs on flinty footing. He twisted around, braced for an attack from the rear. Were they coming in behind now? Over the barrel of his gun, as he lay, flat and grim, he saw a rider less than 100 yards away coming up the valley at a trot from the creek. He held the rider in his sights, hesitated, and lowered the carbine as he saw the man's hands were free of weapons. What sort of business was this? At the same time, the firing from the ridge had not been resumed. The horseman came on, oblivious to the life and death act being played here. Watching keenly, Durand gave a short exclamation of surprise. The rider was a woman!

Thinking of the guns on the ridge, he frantically tried to wave her back. The pot-shooting boys behind him couldn't be expected to miss a second victim. Yet a thick, wondering silence continued to grip the valley and the oncoming rider continued to ignore his signs and came on unconcernedly. As Durand looked again at the ridge, four men, two of them aiding a limping companion, disappeared over the top. So they were clearing out. The coming of this woman, this girl, had been his luck today, and he got up on his feet to face her.

This day had been jammed with the unexpected, but he was unprepared for what he saw: a slim young woman with surprisingly cool, yet friendly, gray eyes. A mighty good-looking young woman, he decided quickly, looked down at him with concern and gravity.

"You took a foolish chance, riding up here like this," Durand told her with reproach. "They're over the hill now, but they've been after me all afternoon." He looked back at the ridge again, half expecting to see the riflemen reappear. It was still empty of men and he turned back to her and reminded her: "I still say you took a long chance."

"I'll remember the lecture," she murmured, and he unconsciously liked her half smile and the way her eyes laughed back at him as she dismounted. He became aware of chestnut hair and a brown, oval face, delicately featured but strong. She wore a calfskin vest over a white blouse, buckskin riding skirt, and the smallest boots he'd ever seen.

She exclaimed over the loss of his horse and told him: "I was out for a ride and heard the shots. I crossed the creek for a better look, then decided to come on closer and I guess they thought there might be others with me."

Her name, he learned after he made his known, was Ellen Winston and she lived at Red Cloud.

"You didn't say where you're from," she said.

"Sometimes it's a good idea not to be from anywhere," he observed with a slow smile.

"I shouldn't have asked that question. It's not considered good manners these days."

She gave him a low laugh and he saw the corners of her eyes crinkle. Her sense of humor, he was discovering, was sharp. "Nobody seems to be from anywhere in particular if you do get an answer," she went on, "but many of them are going somewhere . . . in a hurry."

Durand looked ruefully at his horse. "If I was in a hurry, which I wasn't exactly, I'm slowed down now."

"I'll ride you to Red Cloud," she offered.

"Thanks, and I'll take it," he answered, and moved to salvage his gear from the dead animal, freeing the cinch and depositing saddle, blanket, and bridle under a rock up the ridge where they couldn't be spotted by a rider traveling the trail. His other belongings he wrapped in a long, yellow slicker to take with him.

"I see you travel light," she observed.

For a girl, he thought, she was keenly observant and seemed aware of the habits of men on the dodge. He replied: "Yes, it's handy and quick if you're in a hurry."

He saw her look at him closely. "I guess it's getting fashionable in this part of the country," she added.

Durand passed up comment on that observation to ask: "How far to this place you call Red Cloud?"

"About six miles."

"Not far. I'm thirsty and hungry. But first I'm going back to that creek for water."

"You can ride behind me."

She mounted easily, kicked her small left boot free from the stirrup, and he swung up behind her with the slicker under one arm. Her horse, he soon noticed, was a saddler and reached out smoothly down the trail under the double load. When they came to the creek, he dismounted while she watered the horse. Conscious of cramped shoulder muscles, he stepped to a place above the ford where the rocks spread out, low and flat. He took off his weather-scoured hat, showing dark hair, thick and matted with sweat, and bent down for his drink. He drank long and deeply, like a plainsman who often goes long without water and relishes each drop, bending shoulders over outspread hands anchored on the flat rocks. When he straightened up, at last, his face glistened with water, which he wiped off with his sleeve. He rolled a cigarette with rapid twists before coming back to where she waited, mounted. He drew the smoke into his lungs hungrily, and, when he turned to her, a half smile creased his wide mouth and his eyes followed her.

"I'm ready if you are," he said.

Durand swung up behind her again and they jogged northwest, back up the valley that had almost been a deathtrap, past Durand's dead horse, and up over the ridge's rim. Losing the horse had fired him like the jab of a Spanish spur, and, when they topped the rise and the country lay spread out before them, he looked again for horsemen, although figuring he would see none.

She reined up, asking: "Do you want to look around?"

He shook his head. "No, I'll get a fresh horse in Red Cloud and come back."

But he did inspect the rough, brush-littered slopes where the killers had hidden, and, as he looked down where his horse lay in the valley, he marveled how he had survived. They were both looking down and the puzzlement in his mind bobbed up as if he were thinking aloud. "I've been shot at before, but this is the first time I never had an idea what it was all about. I'm still trying to figure out why they jumped me. It don't make sense, unless they got the wrong man. Have any ideas? You know the country."

"If I did, I'd tell you," she said soberly. "A lot of things don't make sense in the Territory. There's no law to speak of

14

below the Kansas line and hardly any above it. That may be exaggerated, but it's close to the truth. With all that, there's bound to be some ambushing, hold-ups, and just plain killings. We have a little of each around Red Cloud, but the bad men let the town pretty much alone because they can come and go there without much trouble."

"You mean it's an outlaw hang-out?"

"Not exactly. The town happens to be the only trading point for a hundred miles for Territory riders and it's just inside the Kansas line. You might say it's just the location, though a sort of sanctuary in a way."

"Well," Durand said, "I'd've been good meat for the buzzards right now if you hadn't busted up the party planned for me. That puts me in your debt. I'll want to hang around Red Cloud a while to make up for it."

"Maybe you won't like the town. I don't think you will."

"Why not?"

The warmth of her voice seemed to have ebbed, replaced by a strange coldness that surprised him. "You won't like it," she said decisively, "unless you're like the men who come there."

"I'd have to look them over to see which bunch I belong to," he countered evasively. "Red Cloud may not like me. So it may be the other way around."

She fell silent and he pondered her words. They might constitute a warning, he thought, wondering at her sudden, tight-lipped silence. Yet he was more puzzled by the mysterious attempt to ambush him and how the mere appearance of a young woman riding onto the scene by chance would disperse four determined men armed with high-powered rifles. He swept the thought away as ungallant, but it occurred to him there might be a possible connection between her and the would-be killers, that they knew her. But if that were true, why had she stopped to help him? Old warning signals flashed through him, and, as these questions remained unanswered, he caught the faint perfume of her hair, swept back softly under her hat by the wind, and he was aware of the slender outline of her body riding lightly in the saddle in front of him. Both had lapsed into silence as they sighted the dark, spread-out cluster on the prairie that was Red Cloud. Durand, the manhunter, sensed oddly that the town posed a lurking challenge to him, to his guns, and he forced himself to push aside and ignore the subtle softness existing in the presence of this pretty young woman who had befriended him, and then coldly dropped a vague warning that a man might take two ways.

Chapter Two

The frontier had touched Red Cloud fleetingly, breathed life into its awkward roots, and marched on swiftly into the bronzed sunset, leaving behind a town that would never be another Dodge City, an Abilene, or an Oglala, but one that, on certain days, was wild as a marauding prairie wolf. Now its main street lay like a twisting stream of grayish dust, its board buildings and sheds and corrals standing like gaunt, gray outposts on the great land that sloped up to the Flints in massive rolls. But when the big, Territory herds moved to shipping points in Kansas, Red Cloud regained a large measure of its old jauntiness and vigor, like a veteran war horse that lifts its head and becomes once more alert, eyes flashing, hoofs stamping, when distant bugles blow. Saloons ran full blast, the red-eye flowed, the town's few merchants smiled as money jingled, and Old Cal Winston, who ran the Western Star Hotel, dusted out his rooms and turned a fresh page on the ink-smeared register. Afterward, the town would settle down into its dust and heat and lethargy and wait sluggishly for another herd to bring its injection of economic energy.

Walt Durand's practiced eyes, roving over Main Street's traffic of horses, men, and buggies, found the prairie settlement obviously enjoying one of its better days. Tie racks were crowded with fagged and beaten horses in front of saloons and stores, an occasional wagon rattled down the street, and trail herd riders moved in and out of the bars to sluice the dust from their throats. At sight of the bustling town, Ellen Winston's cold mood seemed to pass and her friendliness returned as suddenly as it had vanished.

They dismounted at Red Cloud's main livery stable, and,

as a boy took the horse, she said: "You can put up at our place if you like."

Durand looked at her steadily, studying her, saw only an open, friendly invitation that any ordinary, hard-riding cowboy would undoubtedly receive. He readily accepted. The hotel, she explained lightly, wasn't much, but it was all the town had, and it was clean and had its dining room. She might have added that, to men slipping out from Indian Territory for a brief brush with civilization, the hotel with its clean bedding and food constituted rare comforts.

As they walked toward the hotel, Durand noted several Texas brands on horses, and some outfits scattered around the Fort Reno area. Few loungers cluttered the boardwalk, for a vast restlessness blew along the street. Men were coming or going with some definite object in mind and there wasn't time to sit in the sun and loaf for an afternoon.

The Western Star, with its weather-stained front, its verandah with sagging chairs and rail scarred by spurred feet, wasn't unlike other plains hotels Durand had seen, except this one, despite its worn appearance and surroundings, had retained a certain durable pride. The pride, he figured, could be laid to a woman's hand. As they went into the hotel, Durand paused to thank the young woman again, and, as he did so, the smile he had seen earlier in the day reappeared. It transformed Ellen into a totally different person; it lit up her face and the doubt and concern were gone now.

Durand signed the register in a slanting hand and went upstairs, his boots bringing sighs from the ancient wooden stairs beneath the thin carpet. In his room, he washed up, rolled a smoke, and rested before going down to supper. He idly considered the room and its worn carpet, the scarred bureau holding the white pitcher and bowl, the old iron bedstead, and the faded framed print of General Robert E. Lee astride

Traveler hanging on the wall. Yet the room was clean and comfortable and offered him more than he was accustomed to most of the time. As he sat in the room's decrepit rocker and finished his cigarette, Ellen Winston stuck in his mind, and he remembered the perfume of her hair, how she handled her horse, and how she sat the saddle.

Finally hunger bit into him and he went down to the hotel's small dining room, taking a chair where he could watch the door. The place was crowded with hungry men. Ellen Winston took his order and he watched her, a slender, trim figure, as she moved about the dining room. He ate with the hunger of a man tired of his plain, campsite cooking, and later he bought the makings from the clerk in the cramped lobby and went outside to the verandah. The sun had dropped behind the dark line of the land and a southeasterly wind was stirring, bringing a softness after the day's hard sunlight.

There he met Cal Winston, Ellen's father, a heavy-set, congenial man in his middle sixties, white-haired and mustached, who sat alone.

"You had a close call," Winston said at length, and, when Durand looked up in surprise, the older man added: "Ellen told me about it." He leaned forward, his pipe in his hand. "I can't think of an explanation for it, but, if I was you, I'd be damned careful in Red Cloud tonight. It looks quiet and peaceful around here just now, but this town has its man for breakfast right regular. Sure as hell there'll be a shootin' tonight. Just give these cowhands time to get likkered up. Now tonight we got a boom town here . . . like some mining camps I've seen . . . but by tomorrow, when the herds move on, she'll be deader'n a week-old flapjack."

Aware that Winston was curious about him, but that etiquette held him back, Durand remarked: "I'm looking for a job. Not in much of a hurry yet. May tie up with some outfit after I've looked around a while."

"Everybody needs hands, even bad ones. You won't have to look far. Just ride up to a cowman and tell him you want to work."

"I'm also looking for a friend of mine," Durand added. "Believe he stayed here at your hotel. Maybe you know him . . . Larry Cramer, big, tall man, talks like a Texan."

The old man chewed on his pipe stem. "I remember him, sure. He was the only guest I had for a few days before the cowmen came to town. I never forget a name or face."

As Durand cupped a match in his hands to light a cigarette, he saw Winston eyeing him closely. Then Durand asked: "Any idea where he is? Or why he left here?"

"He checked out three days ago, if I recollect right. Didn't say where he was goin' and ain't been back since. He was friendly enough, but never talked about himself."

"That's a little odd," Durand said. "He said he'd meet me here. By this afternoon for certain. He was a man who kept his word, hell or high water. I expected to be talking to him here tonight."

"Maybe it is a little strange, come to think of it. Might've had an accident . . . maybe a horse fell with him. But I wouldn't get worried about him till tomorrow. Give him time." Winston's voice had sharpened with interest, or was it fear, something akin to that strange, unexpected change he had sensed in Ellen Winston that afternoon?

"It's not likely that he had an accident or that he'd be late," Durand said doggedly. "It's against his nature to say he'd be here, then not to show up." Durand might have added that, in his letter, Cramer said he would be in Red Cloud for certain a day before the day set for the meeting in order not to miss Durand.

Then Durand pressed another question at Winston. "See

him with anybody here you know?"

"No," came the quick answer, almost too quickly, Durand thought. "He always seemed to be on the move, always riding in and out of town. Like he knew where he was goin' or had a chore to do. A right pleasant fellow, too, but he wasn't here for any sight-seeing trip, you could see that."

"That's Larry Cramer, all right."

After that, the talk fell off and they smoked in silence. Winston relit his pipe, shifted uneasily in his chair, and stared out into the darkened street as though he were thinking heavily. Durand sat silently, feeling that there was more to be said if he waited long enough. From down the street came the sounds of early evening, of men and horses moving. A few feet away, Winston pulled noisily at his pipe. Then abruptly, as if making a decision, he rose to his feet and walked the length of the verandah, looking searchingly into the shadows. When he returned, he sat down heavily, leaned over until Durand heard his heavy, rapid breathing. Winston was ready to tell him something.

"I'll say this," Winston said in a low voice, "but it's a damned lie if you repeat it. The day before your friend pulled out, I saw him talkin' to Matt Braden. First time I ever saw the two of 'em together. They stood right over there in front of the door. I was in the lobby, couldn't miss them. Braden said something and Cramer answered him real sharp. That was all. They stood there glarin' at each other . . . then walked away. The next morning Cramer rode out of town carrying a Winchester. He was loaded for bear. He hasn't showed up since."

Durand's voice cut like a knife across Winston's words: "And who's Matt Braden?"

"He's the king of this whole country and he rules with an iron hand." Words came rushing now, as if Durand had

21

broken down a vast flood of reticence dammed up in the older man over a long period of time. It was as if the quick knowledge that Durand stood on the other side of the fence from the powerful Braden, that fact alone, had ripped away Winston's customary reserve and silence. And Durand let the man talk.

Winston leaned forward in his chair. "Braden came in here from western Kansas with a big roll of money five years ago. He didn't say how he came by it and nobody cared to ask him how he got it. He prospered fast. When he ain't runnin' Red Cloud, he ramrods a big outfit up in the Flints. That's what the boys say. Nobody I know has ever been up there and lived to tell it. Nobody seems to know where it is, for some reason, and to be truthful nobody is lookin' for it. . . . Now I been on the frontier from Montana to North Texas, an' laid eyes on a herd of gun slingers, but those hands of Braden's learned to exercise their trigger fingers long before they threw a loop . . . or I miss my guess. I don't say Braden himself has killed any ranchers around here. That I don't know. But he's hard as a boulder and won't stand for nobody to cross him."

Winston drew back, carefully inspected the shadows again, and murmured: "Ellen told me a little more than it might've appeared she knew. Luck was with you today, Durand. That bunch of hired killers was from Red Cloud, though I can't say they're Braden's riders." With that, Winston got up. "Now that I've had my say, I will go up to bed and rest my feet. My advice to you is stay out of the dark."

As Durand, still pondering what he had heard, murmured his thanks, old Cal Winston knocked the ashes from his pipe on the railing and clumped inside to go upstairs.

For a while Durand looked down the street, watching yellow splashes of light break from the saloons and listening to sounds of noisy, growing revelry. Men swung along the street and occasionally a rider jogged past, saddle leather creaking. Across from the hotel in a darkened house, a woman's high, brittle voice rose in sudden anger; a door slammed, shooting its flat, sharp break into the soft night, and booted feet tramped across wooden flooring. Far down the street, to the east, a gun *cracked,* men shouted, and a horse launched a quick, pounding journey out of town, south toward the Territory. Red Cloud, made virile again, was in the throes of a lusty night and there would be no let-up until near daylight. Tomorrow night or the next, after the riders had returned to their herds, coyotes would howl their brief threnody after sundown, and there would be a hollow silence running along the deserted street.

Durand finished his cigarette and started toward the saloons as he found himself suddenly restless and disinclined to sit the evening out at the hotel. At the noisy Osage Girl, which appeared to attract the largest clientele, he stepped inside, into the brightness and din and smoke. Cowmen hugged the long, polished bar, which ran the length of the low frame building. At the opposite wall men thronged around a faro game. Toward the rear of the establishment someone pounded a tuneless piano with whiskey-driven gusto, while the shuffling of booted feet almost drowned out the music as cowpunchers cavorted and swayed with red-lipped dancing partners. With all this was the pungent smell of raw liquor, rolling tobacco smoke, and sweating bodies.

Durand strolled to the bar and called for whiskey. In his travel-marked clothes he attracted little attention, and the line along the bar settled back after a brief inspection. The whiskey warmed him and he had another, his quota for the night. Reaching for his tobacco, he looked at the crowd as mirrored in the huge glass behind the bar. Beside him he heard a man tell his companion: "Braden's bunch is in town tonight. Reckon there's a little easy meat around somewhere."

Durand stayed there half an hour, listening to vague talk, smoking, and looking at the crowd. Tiring of the fruitless game, he stepped outside and sauntered slowly eastward, thinking hard, prodded by a great restlessness. Larry Cramer's absence concerned him more than he liked to admit, and in his mind he turned over in careful detail all that Cal Winston had told him half fearfully in the shadows of the hotel. He felt genuinely disturbed over his friend and a rising premonition of trouble continued to grip him, refusing to be pushed aside, and he longed to translate thinking into action. However, there was nothing he could do until daybreak. He decided there was more to Winston's words than a mere account to a stranger of a turbulent cow town and the man who dominated it. The story had been intended as a warning, he was sure of that.

Durand went farther along the meandering street, saw it offered him nothing, and decided to rest tonight and make discreet inquiries tomorrow. So he turned back in the direction of the hotel. The boardwalk echoed fewer footsteps now as the night advanced; saloons would be roaring for hours to come.

Durand found the hotel verandah deserted and again he recalled Winston's warning. Advancing through the doorway, he heard talk, marked by a woman's pleasant voice, directly before him. First a man's bulky figure loomed in the low lamplight coming from the lobby and beside the man Durand saw Ellen Winston. Durand, apparently unnoticed as yet, moved to step aside to allow them to pass through the narrow doorway out onto the deserted porch, when the man, his head turned to the girl, bumped him lightly. As the other stepped back, Durand caught the instant challenge in the man's alert face. Ellen glanced up in surprise, then recognized Durand, who heard her speak their names as she introduced the men.

The other man was Matt Braden. The name threw Durand taut and tense; it swirled through his mind, to cling there, heating him with a steady interest. They shook hands briefly, without warmth, carefully, each sizing up the other. And instead of passing on as Durand expected, Braden asked boldly: "Looking for a job?"

"Maybe . . . if it's with the right outfit."

Braden's expressions switched from the cursory inspection he had been giving Durand to one of abrupt, deeper interest, mingled with faint amusement. The man's tremendous strength was evident at a glance. There was a boundless power lurking in the enormous shoulders, the massive hands, the strong head, and dark, broad face, the heavy, compelling voice. Here was a giant, muscled man who drove himself hard and would demand equally exacting perfection from men serving under him. Here, Durand thought, was a personality as untamed and unfettered as the wildest border haunt; here stood a supreme test for any man who might seek to test his speed with guns.

Now Braden was saying in a rich, dominating voice: "If you can throw a rope and know how to take care of yourself, see my foreman, Red Kane, at the Osage Girl. You'll want to ride with the top outfit if you work in this part of the country. Think it over."

Without waiting for an answer, and perhaps not expecting one, the broad man moved away, taking the girl's arm and passing outside as Durand stood aside. Looking after them, Durand saw them merge with the shadows and step down into the street, his mind alive with the likeness of the man with whom Larry Cramer had quarreled. Pressing, too, but only for the moment, was the question of Braden's possessiveness with the girl. The man would be possessive and dominating with any woman.

Then Durand turned and went up to his room. In the thin light of a single lamp, he inspected his Colts, partly from long habit, partly from a need to keep his hands busy while he thought hard. The guns were in perfect condition, he knew, but he cleaned and reloaded them. He had never taken chances with his guns and he did not propose to relax this longstanding habit now, for the Colts were all that stood between him and oblivion. His venture to Red Cloud was sliding into familiar' grooves, he thought, and those grooves were guns. He hoped he would see the day when he could hang them up to rust, or fling them from him to the rocky bottom of a creek.

But in his mind, outlined clearly, was the image of Larry Cramer, and the guns had a job to perform, perhaps. Where was Larry? He'd have to find out. At last, Durand removed his boots, sat in the rocking chair, and rolled a smoke. Facing the open window, he stared unseeingly into the subdued, shadowed street below, with Matt Braden's dark, mocking face strongly before him.

Chapter Three

A little past daylight, Durand came downstairs to the lobby of the Western Star where he found Denton, the thin, yawning clerk, the lone early morning occupant. Durand went over to the desk and asked bluntly: "What can you tell me about Larry Cramer?"

The clerk's thin face, roused from its drowsiness, showed surprise. "You a friend of his?"

Durand nodded. "That's why I'm interested."

The man flipped a page on the register, running a skinny finger down the list of names. "According to this," he said dryly, "he checked out three days ago."

"I know that. What I want to know is did he drop a hint where he might be going?"

Resentment suddenly edged the clerk's mouth, and his small eyes narrowed. "He didn't tell me. All I know is what the book shows. I don't keep tab on every guest. They come and go pretty fast around here."

Durand was persistent. "That's all you know about him, then?"

The clerk nodded, eyes hostile.

In an even voice, Durand asked: "What about mail? Did he get any?"

"I don't remember."

Now Durand stared coldly at the man behind the desk, turned deliberately, and walked slowly out to the verandah, aware of eyes boring into his back. So far, he told himself while he smoked and waited for breakfast, Cal Winston was the only friendly man he had met in Red Cloud.

Soon afterward, when he entered the dining room, he saw

Ellen Winston at her breakfast duties. He spoke to her and she nodded. While he ate his bacon and eggs and biscuits, she stayed either in the kitchen or busied herself with other customers. He left money for his breakfast, retrieved his hat, and quit the hotel. The clerk had turned around from behind the desk to watch him as he passed out, a tall man with deliberate movements.

Red Cloud still slept in its exhaustion from the night before. Swinging saloon doors were motionless; tie racks stood empty. Durand's boots made a hollow, echoing sound on the boardwalk.

Sandy-moustached Luke Givins, smoking in front of his livery stable, saw a tall man striding evenly down Red Cloud's deserted Main Street in the stillness of early morning. Presently he recognized the man who had ridden in behind Ellen Winston the day before. Probably a drifter, a tramp peeler. Luke had wondered about that, but, being wise, he hadn't asked any questions. It wasn't good manners in Red Cloud to pry into a man's business unless you knew him well, and then sometimes it was poor judgment. By keeping his mouth shut, Givins had managed to get along in the town.

When Durand came up, Givins looked as uninterested as if he hadn't seen this early-morning riser, although the two were the only men on the street. Durand saw a little man in his late fifties, wiry and alert, with eyes that were cautious, yet friendly. Givins waited patiently for the other to state his business.

"I need two horses," Durand said. "One pack animal."

"Got what you need," Givins said, and turned inside the stable runway, Durand following.

Later, with no further words spoken between them other than the rental fee for the horses, Durand rode away, leading a pack horse, heading southeast. Givins watched him with undisciplined interest now as rider and horses were lost from sight when the land dipped. *He shore don't talk much,* Givins concluded, *but he seems to know where he's goin'.*

Durand rode steadily into the sun. There was still a left-over of night coolness hanging in the air and the ride quick-ened his senses, sharpening him. He set a brisk pace until he spied the line of hills overlooking the attempted ambuscade. Riding closer, he saw buzzards circling and diving below the line of the hills, down into the small valley where the dead horse lay. He rode straight over the rim and into the valley. His gear lay where he had cached it, and he threw blanket, saddle, and bridle on the pack animal. Remounting, he rode up the stony slope to the top, where he got down and in-spected the ground with care. Looking down into the valley for a moment, he wondered again how he had escaped. He re-membered that even good riflemen sometimes miss their tar-gets when firing from a height.

Carefully he worked from left to right, until he found all four positions the gunmen had held. Two of the men had hidden in heavy brush, which covered the slope like a thick mat. The other two had chosen rock barricades. Empty rifle cartridges, boot marks, and numerous cigarette stubs marked each hiding place. Judging from marks left in each position, it occurred to him that they had waited for him long before he rode blindly within range of their spitting rifles.

By noon Durand was back at the stable and had switched his saddle to a rangy Spanish horse Givins brought up from a rear corral. For a while they squatted silently in the slanting shade of a shed and smoked. His eyes on the horse, Givins re-marked with appreciation: "There's the best hoss around here for travelin'. You can't wear him down . . . tough as raw-hide. An' I don't let him out to just anybody."

"Why'd you let me have him?" Durand asked softly. "I'm a stranger."

"In one way you are," the liveryman agreed. "In another you ain't. Remember you came in town with Miss Winston. I reckon that gives you a clean bill."

"Never thought of that."

"She's purty particular about her company, I might add, 'cept for this fellow Braden, who's courtin' her heavy, or tryin' to. Folks around town here are wonderin' how long she'll hold out against him. A big bull like that pesters the life. . . ."

Givins paused, as if he suddenly remembered something; his voice faltered. He looked through the stable door out toward the street like a man who knows he has spoken out of turn. But when he turned back to Durand, both men grinned simultaneously. Givins said critically: "That's the first time I ever let a remark like that slip about Braden. Must be gettin' old an' thick-headed. Talk like that is bad medicine in this man's town. First thing I know Kane or Crawford'll come in here gunnin' for me."

"Who's that?"

"Braden's boys," Givins said briefly, wanting to dismiss the subject. He returned to the Spanish horse, scanning the long mane and sweeping tail in open admiration with the intent of a man who loves horses. "A man rode through here not long ago with a hoss kinda like this one. I tried to buy him, but he just laughed at me. Said he'd just as soon sell a leg or arm. . . ."

Durand had risen to his feet. He stood there looking fixedly at Givins. "What was his name . . . Cramer?"

Givins rubbed his chin and nodded reflectively. "Believe it was. He stabled his hoss here when he wasn't on the move. Sometimes he'd load up a pack hoss and head out. Four or five days later he'd come back, rest up, and start out again. I was curious about him, but I never ask a man his business." He pursed his mouth, calculating. "It's been four days now since he was in here."

For the third time since he had come to Red Cloud, Durand asked the question that was yet unanswered, and Luke Givins said: "Sometimes he headed west or east when he left town. But the last time he went due north. I remember because I offered to buy his mount again and I watched him ride on a beeline for the Flints."

North for the Flints, Durand thought. Maybe north for the Flints and Braden's hang-out, the trouble spot that had drawn them both to this powder keg south Kansas border town.

"The man with the Spanish horse," Durand said grimly, "was a friend of mine. You may never see that horse again."

He left the shed, Givins looking after him searchingly, and started for the hotel. He had planned to question the stable proprietor about Larry today, but the man's unlooked for voluntary story had cleared up that problem in a hurry. Durand had also discovered a man who did not knuckle down to Braden. He guessed he could thank Ellen Winston for the unexpected show of friendship and confidence; otherwise, the little man would have remained silent before a stranger. He regretted his parting remark about the horse. Yet when he thought of Larry, it was with the old, heavy, insistent premonition that had clung to him since he had reached the town and encountered its dark, brooding undercurrent.

Halfway to the hotel, he met Ellen Winston as she emerged from a store, her arms filled with bundles. For an instant, he thought she would walk past him without speaking. However, she turned to him and he helped with her packages as they moved along the street, where horse traffic still stirred only sluggishly.

"You seem in a hurry," she observed, walking faster to keep pace with his long strides.

He muttered his apology and slowed down. "I rode out and got my gear," he said. "Now I'm going out again." He caught the question in her eyes but left it unanswered.

As if from a great distance, although they walked side-by-side, he heard her say: "Come and visit us tonight." She walked with her eyes lightly upon him and she noted the effect of her words on him, saw him search her face. He almost halted on the boardwalk as he said: "Thank you. But I won't be here."

She resisted an impulse to ask where he was going, when he would return. Instead, she asked: "You'll be back?"

"I expect to."

They walked silently along after that. When they entered the hotel, where he and Braden had collided the night before, it came to him that the big man probably would be here again tonight, swaggering a little, his heavy voice cutting through the darkness.

Cal Winston nodded over his two-week-old newspaper from his seat in the dingy lobby and went back to his reading, his old eyes squinting at the small print. Ellen moved away then, and, as Durand climbed the stairs to his room, Denton threw a swift upward glance at him as he looked up from the desk. After taking shells from his belongings, Durand came back down, spurs jangling, nodded at the absorbed Winston, and started from the lobby.

From inside the dining room, Ellen saw his tall form fill the doorway and hesitate momentarily as he looked up and down the street with a caution that stemmed from long habit. When, through the window opening on the verandah, she glimpsed him pass on down the street, she stood there thinking about him a little regretfully. *What moved this man? Why was he so close-mouthed and distant, yet friendly?* Frankly he puzzled her. Many riders who stayed overnight at the hotel were wary men, men who looked behind them with the alertness of a suspicious wild animal, men with the indelible stamp of the hunted on their lean, taut faces, men who rode south in a hurry early the next morning for deep in the Territory. Walt Durand was wary, too, she had learned when he sat where he could see the men passing through the dining room door. But with all that, there was a certain ease to his movements, as though he feared no one, and there was a half-hidden courtliness to his manners that belied his sometimes cold voice as when he dismissed Braden's job offer, and, too, there was a mystery about him that heightened her interest, caused her to speculate about where he had come from, what drew him to a tough cow town like Red Cloud, why his eyes roved ceaselessly.

She still stood there, absorbed in her thoughts, when her father came in for his dinner. "Just another cowboy, Ellen," he said teasingly, "just another cowboy. The plains are full of 'em."

She flushed. "What cowboy do you have in mind?"

"The one who just went out the door."

She became suddenly indignant and demanded: "Can't a woman look at a man, talk to him, without involving herself?"

"Sure." Her father laughed. "But it don't pay to get interested in a man who's liable to be a corpse."

"What do you mean?" she flung the words at him.

"Why, it's plain as daylight at noon, Ellen, he's lookin' for a friend of his and this friend is missin'. His friend, that fellow Cramer who stayed with us, off and on, didn't like Braden. They had words outside here the night before Cramer left.

Now Durand is out lookin' for 'is friend." Cal Winston put his arm around his daughter, his voice lowered: "Remember the Nebraska man who disappeared, and the friend who came in here huntin' him. He didn't come back, either. However, I got an idea Durand knows the fundamentals of handlin' a six-gun. It's plain to me that ambush you pulled him out of wasn't accidental. Somebody's out to get him sure. Probably Braden's boys. They wasn't indulgin' in target practice, though I guess those four killers needed it, from the results they got. Four against one ought to be easy for the big side. But it wasn't that time." He chuckled; the thought pleased him.

"What makes you think Matt is mixed up in this?" Ellen was doubtful, questioning her father's accusations.

"I see and hear a lot of things you never know about," he reminded her wisely. "Things a woman never hears."

"But Matt has been kind to us in many ways."

Winston's face tightened. "He owns everything in this town but you and me and the hotel. He'll be kind till he gets what he wants." Winston sat down heavily in a chair. "Naturally a man's kind to the woman he wants to marry. He shows her his best manners, his best side. You can learn more about a man from his saloon pals than you can from the women he hasn't got."

Ellen wheeled away and went back to the kitchen. Winston, his shoulders sagging as he leaned against the table, sent worried eyes after her, observing with the wisdom of older years that she didn't believe all he had said. A woman, especially a good woman, had to see it as an act before her, he guessed. As he looked after her, he remembered from back over the years a slender girl with gray eyes and chestnut hair of whom Ellen was the image. He remembered a young wife whose faith was strong and immovable. He remembered a little town sprawled on the endless Dakota prairies where he and a handful of friends had dug a grave in the frozen ground. There had been many towns since, none of them good, all of the same hard pattern. *And Ellen,* he reflected, *is as headstrong as her mother. You had to prove a thing to her.* . . . Several cowmen came into the dining room and he swept the thoughts aside.

Down the street, Durand entered MacGregor's General Merchandise Store and bought a small supply of grub. Walking along the dusty street, with the sun burning into him, he caught curious glances from the few men lounging in front of the saloons. The town had been emptied of its fast-traveling visitors like a circus tent after the last act.

Inside the stable, he began making up the pack for the second animal and checking the short Winchester. Givins watched him keenly, aware of the expert interest the tall rider showed in the condition of his rifle.

"It pays to be prepared," Givins remarked.

"I've found that out."

"Any chore I can do for you." The man's warm friendliness caught Durand again. He had become positive of his stand while they talked at the shed. Here was a man he could trust.

Durand said: "Nothing I know of, thanks. I aim to be gone a day or two. Got to find out some things I can't learn here. The first is Larry Cramer."

"There's one warnin' I'm passin' on to you," said Givins, his voice lowered. "If you run into Braden's bunch, look out for this here Red Kane, his foreman. He's a slick hand with a gun. About the fastest I ever saw. He's killed three men I know of around Red Cloud, an' the Lord knows how many before he tied in with Braden. He's not a cowman . . . he's a born killer, loves to look over his gun barrels an' see a man wither an' die. I seen two of his local killin's. An' there's Smoke Crawford and Cash Edmund. They came in here with Kane. All of the same litter, I'd say. Maybe not as vicious as Kane, but they've killed men an' they'll kill more. The rest of Braden's outfit is just mill-run outlaws.

"I don't sleep around campfires," said Durand. "I'll remember what you said." He swung into the saddle and, leading the pack horse, rode out into the searing heat. Luke Givins's sharp eyes ranged after him, then, with a feeling of caution and apprehension, he looked back up the street. Several men were also peering after the horseman traveling east.

When Durand reached the ambush site, he tied the horses to low-growing brush in the scant shade of a stubby jack oak. And patiently, with the care of a man used to tracking, he covered the ground above the rim of the hills until he found where the killers' horses had been tied among a clump of trees hidden from the trail that ran east and west. An object in the sun-yellowed grass caught his eyes. He bent over and picked up a man's bloody handkerchief. He remembered then the man who had been helped over the ridge when Ellen Winston appeared in the valley. From here, Durand saw, the men's trail struck boldly north. He went back to his horses, mounted quickly, and followed the tracks, aware of a tingling inside his body. He was on a cold trail but there would be an end to it and he would find it.

Four hours later he pulled up in a shaded draw where a clear spring fed giant cottonwoods. Cattle tracks marked the ground around the water hole. Here the foursome had stopped, smoked, and ridden on northward, deeper into the frowning hills. To the north the land rose gradually into larger hills, some of them massive, slashed by deep valleys and heavy timber. Bleached limestone outcroppings were revealed on the higher areas and the grass grew rich. He watered the horses and rode ahead, avoiding high ridges where he would be outlined.

At dusk he made camp at the edge of a short stretch of grassland near a shallow creek. He staked the saddle horse on a lariat, hobbled the packer, cooked supper, and then took his blankets atop a hill where he could watch the horses and the back trail. The tracks were becoming more difficult to follow in the limestone country, but so far he had not lost them. Here and there iron hoofs had scraped against rocks or dug into soft soil or the tall grass showed the path of a horse.

Darkness fell like a thick mantle, but lightened somewhat after stars made their pale glimmer. He could make out dimly the dark shapes of the horses and hear them pulling at the rich grass that grew waist high to a man in places. There was the steady chorus of insects, the call of night birds. Durand was restless despite the long ride and his right hand strayed inside his shirt until he felt the coolness of metal. He unpinned the object and held it firmly in his hand, pressing its sharp edges against his palm. It was a U.S. marshal's badge and the feel of it raked over old memories. The picture of Larry Cramer rose before him with a warmness and clarity that seemed real in the hill darkness. Durand was not superstitious, but he thought he was on the verge of discovering something about his missing friend. He had followed the trail with that feeling urging him ahead. And there were other memories as he lay in his blankets—Ellen Winston's wide, gray eyes, her soft voice; his own father, a tall man who had ridden out of Fort Abraham Lincoln during a Sioux campaign in the late 1860s as a civilian scout, never to return; his father talking to him, a boy, about Durand's mother; how he had hung on the words about the woman who was a wistful memory to her son; how, at ten, he had started living with a kindly frontier family and at fourteen had ventured out on his own, and with it all a certain loneliness he had never erased from his being. He had drifted into the Southwest, back north, and then to Kansas. At Caldwell he had thrown his first gun in a street fight. Men said he had his father's knack for guns and tracking. By the time he was twenty-seven, he had officered at Abilene, Hunnewell, and Wichita. For three years now he had made his headquarters at Fort Reno in the Territory. And tonight this was another cold camp in the hills, like many he had shared with Larry Cramer, who had gone to Red Cloud to look into a stolen horse ring operating from the Mexican border to Kansas. With Larry missing, the job loomed larger, half sinister. A drowsiness crept over him. He stuck the badge back inside his shirt and slept with dark shadows haunting him, a girl's face in the background.

Chapter Four

Some time during the night Durand awoke. Out of the darkness
a foreign noise had aroused him. Six-gun in hand, he raised up
in his blankets, eyes searching the land around the hill. The sky
was lighter now and he spotted the horses. He tensed as he saw
the saddle animal raise his head and look in the direction of the
creek. Then the horse shied suddenly away, the lariat trailing.
Checked when the rope tightened at full length, the animal
stamped nervously, still suspicious of what lay beyond the dark
wall of the tree-lined creek.

From Durand's post atop the hill, he could look down on
the creek; to his left timber grew thickly. He peered patiently
into the dark mass of trees along the creek, but saw nothing
moving, and presently the saddle horse quieted and went
back to the grass. What had caused the horse to shy away?
The sound stirring Durand had been sharp, like metal against
rock. Below the timber on his left the shallow creek could be
crossed on rocks, he remembered. He crawled from the hill,
then, until the timber hid him. From this angle he was almost
on a level with the creekbank. Under the trees along the bank
he saw moonlight breaking through in patches, but the
shadows were deep and widespread. He decided to cross the
creek by the rocks and scout the far side. Before crossing, he
crouched on the bank to look once again. There was no
movement and he crossed swiftly to the other side. He was
moving from tree to tree, keeping in the shadows, when he
stood stone still. In the distance, there came the unmistak-
able beat of a horse traveling fast. A breath of wind sighed and
moaned through the timber, then heavy, brooding silence.
Durand stalked beyond the creek in a wide circle until the

hills barred his way. He found nothing, so he turned back.

Afterward, he returned to camp to smoke and wait for dawn, when he cooked up a meal in the timber, watered the horses at the creek, and recrossed the creek afoot. In a short time he found what he was seeking—boot prints behind a bush from which could be seen the little meadow where he had pastured the horses. Farther back, he saw where a horse had been tied to a sapling.

By late morning, Durand was forced to admit reluctantly that the trail had petered out. Once the men had ridden nearly a quarter of a mile in the waters of a shallow stream. A little pile of fallen earth where a horse had plunged up a sloping bank put him back on the trail for a short time. Soon afterward the tracks mingled with those of a horse herd, which presently broke up into three separate bands, all traveling in different directions. Doggedly Durand read the blurred signs, deciding to follow one trail north whose chief characteristic was the peculiar, turned-out left forehoof of a horse with particularly wide prints. That imprint, heaviest of the four horses, had reappeared repeatedly since he had first discovered it at the ambush, and so he stalked it until it, too, was lost on a wide plain where many cattle had crossed, obliterating all identifying marks with the thoroughness of a sweeping broom.

Durand pulled up, pondering the countless tracks. He felt powerless and angry at his helplessness. Stubbornly he tackled the task again. For two hours or more he covered the ground with great care, several times dismounting to obtain a closer inspection. But the tracks were completely masked in the churned-up earth and grass left by the herd. There was little hope that he could pick up the tracks farther on, but he rode ahead and entered a narrow cleft in the hills, determined to make a circle in an effort to find a tell-tale print.

Rising on both sides of him now were rock-ribbed hills, opening into a wild, brush-littered sweep of country, wilder than any he had yet seen. Several hundred yards ahead his course widened and he rounded a rocky bend.

Before him, to the north, yawned rolling uplands, rich with grass, to the west, the hills loomed rougher, the timber thicker. He discovered he traveled a well-worn trail, which surprised him, for when he rode into the cleft, only a faint path was revealed. He reined up to study the ground, his interest mounting. When he raised his eyes again, he suddenly grew erect in the saddle and his right, ungloved hand dropped to his gun.

Four horsemen were cantering toward him on the same trail. They appeared to sight him about the same time he saw them. After checking their horses momentarily, they came on boldly, presenting a well-armed, dangerous picture to his practiced eyes. Now Durand caught the glint of sunlight on gun barrels and he shifted in the saddle to give his right arm full freedom. He felt something inside him contract, then grow cold, as he recognized Matt Braden's bulky figure in the lead. Durand waited, weighing his chances in a showdown. As the riders came closer, his attention traveled unerringly to Braden. The man's taste for gaudy finery extended to his hand-carved Mexican saddle, bedecked with silver ornaments, and he made a commanding figure in the saddle. There was something deadly and fierce about him. He was bigger and of more perfect build than Durand had thought from their first short meeting at the hotel. The man's massive shoulders seemed to ripple with muscle, radiating power and tenacity that struck Durand with peculiar force and instinctively caused his blood to run hot. And old warnings, like the tolling of clear-toned bells, rang coldly within him as the riders halted a few yards away.

41

Durand spoke a low greeting, waiting for what might come.

At last Braden said quietly: "A little off the reservation, ain't you?" There was a hint of puzzlement in the question.

"Not that I'm aware of," Durand countered, taking in the others in a sweeping appraisal—a big-boned, red-whiskered man on Braden's right who he took to be Red Kane, a little, lithe, hawk-faced rider, and a nervous, dark gunman with cold, boring eyes, all bearing the rough stamp of border fighters.

"Well," Braden said dryly, "you're on my range land. Since you're not one of my men, I want to know what you're doin' out here."

"I'm looking."

"Lookin' for what?"

Durand let his answer drop roughly, like a warning. "For four bushwhackers."

Braden smiled thinly. "Man, this is ideal country for that kind of work. Maybe you'll find what you're lookin' for. Say, you look to be the man I met at the hotel the other night. That right?"

"Yes. You offered me a job. Remember?"

"The offer still stands. Better jump one way or the other." He paused and looked significantly at Durand. "You're after four men, you say? Chances are you'll never find them. This is wild country, plenty of room, and men disappear easily."

Braden moved to ride on, but Kane spoke up hotly: "Hold on, Matt. Let's talk to this fellow some more. Crawford and Edmund might be interested, too."

Durand couldn't miss the crudely veiled threat, and he read the hot glitter in Kane's eyes. Kane turned to the hawk-faced rider. "Edmund, what do you say?"

Before he could answer, Braden broke in: "Ride on. We've got work to do."

Like a chastened schoolboy, Kane spurred his horse to follow. But as he rode stubbornly away, he flung his sullen anger at Durand: "See you again, snooper!"

As they galloped around the bend, Braden and his foreman, riding close together, appeared to be exchanging heated words. Durand, his tension ebbing, watched their dust settle on the rocky trail before he rode on. Braden's second offer of a job and his abrupt crackdown on the foreman's obviously wild temper stirred him thoughtfully. And where had the riders come from? Their horses looked fresh, which might mean Braden's hidden headquarters lay in this area. The thought quickened him and he resolved to look around.

It was late afternoon and there was a slackening in the harsh punishment meted out by the sun. When the little opening, with its rich grass and curving cottonwoods, rose ahead of him, he pointed directly for it. He had ridden steadily after meeting Braden, but had failed to uncover further horse tracks and there were no signs of a trail leading to a ranch.

Afterward, in somber study, he was to ponder at the turn of events that led him to this shadowed place. He first watered his horses, and then drank his fill from the deep, clear spring, conscious of a great, unbroken stillness. Riding to higher ground on one side of the spring, he saw brush wood for fire. A cluster of saplings, backgrounded by thick brush, attracted him, and he rode that way. At this point, without warning, his horse suddenly jumped aside, jerking the lead rope and burning Durand's hand. The saddle horse's actions were conveyed swiftly to the pack animal, which began pulling wildly on the halter. Durand, his horse quivering under him, scanned the saplings, looked beyond into the brush, and saw only a dead campfire among the trees. Afoot, he advanced alertly through the timber, and he held a gun in his hand. There was nothing suspicious here and he moved into the brush, rustling the dry leaves underfoot. Then, half hidden in the undergrowth, he saw the body of a man, face down in the leaves, one arm flung outward., the other bent grotesquely.

Running forward, Durand looked down, a strange trembling rippling his body. He turned the man over gently with one hand, a quaking fear jolting him. A short cry burst from him. A wild torrent of feeling seized him, shook him with its violence, and the twisted picture of a man's face was engraved in his eyes. The man was Larry Cramer.

Like a man suddenly gone berserk, Durand cursed passionately, softly and loudly, an uncontrollable rage ripping him, and the one thought of revenge burned into his mind like a hot iron. He stalked through the woods, as though there might be gunmen lurking in the brush and lengthening shadows. He would gladly welcome a right to avenge the man who lay silently under the trees. Finally, when he turned to look again, he was sick and despairing, and slowly he began the grim task of examining the tragedy of this last campfire. Larry, he found, had been shot five times—all from behind—and his body dragged from near the campfire into the brush. Durand judged the fire to have been made the day before. He also circled the camp, bent low, eyes shutting over the ground with a newly found fierceness. It was as if all his senses had been sharpened to a razor's edge made marvelously keen by the shock of finding the body. Higher up, where the timber grew thickest, he halted, grunting with surprise at what he found there.

★ ★ ★ ★ ★

The sun was preparing to dive from sight when Durand, with Larry Cramer's body tied in a slicker on the jittery pack horse, left the spring and the tall cottonwoods. *If those trees could talk,* he thought bitterly. The next morning he trotted into the outskirts of Red Cloud and up to Luke Givins's horse barn.

At that moment, Givins came out, leading a horse. "Glad you're back!" he called out cheerfully. "Get off and I'll take them horses. You look. . . ." Givins's eyes fastened on the pack horse's obvious burden. "Is that . . . ?" he began, and stopped, an unspoken question mirrored in his face.

Durand nodded and said: "Larry Cramer." Then bitterly: "Shot in the back! Five times! Never had a chance from what I could see. Found him 'way back in the hills. Brought him in for decent burial so the coyotes and buzzards wouldn't get him."

Givins flashed out angrily: "I was afraid of somethin' like that. It's happened before an' it'll go on till somebody with enough guts and guns cleans out this country."

"You mean . . . ?"

"Yes! Braden an' Kane an' that bunch!"

"I met them."

"The hell you say! What happened?"

"Nothing much. There were four of them. Kane was itching to start a fight, but his boss called him off and offered me a job."

Givins spat into the dust with relief. "Lucky they didn't all four gang you. Now that job offer, it 'pears to me, is just a way to get you where they want you. Braden offers every new rider that comes along a job. That way he can find out about him. If he don't fit in, he can always get rid of him," he explained, looking warningly at Durand. "Meanwhile, if I was in your

45

boots, I'd look twice before I took a seat in front of an open window."

Larry Cramer was buried in a rough pine box that afternoon in Red Cloud's rather large cemetery on the open prairie. After the services, Ellen Winston and her father, Givins and his wife, Durand and the dark-clothed preacher, the Reverend Tom Anderson, walked back to town, a heavy silence hanging over the little group. To Durand, the fact that these people were the only ones in the town who attended attested to their goodness and friendliness for a man who was a stranger and had died alone. It was a touching human quality he would not forget.

When they reached the main part of town, the Givinses took Reverend Anderson home with them to supper and Cal Winston stopped off in a store, leaving Durand and Ellen to walk together to the hotel.

She noticed that, whereas Durand had been grim when he left to search the hills, he now was doubly so, showing a keen, searching hardness that had become a part of him. Even now, as they walked silently along the street, she saw the terrible thoroughness with which he scanned each face, how he observed men across the dusty street, and his manner of watching an incoming rider. It struck her that he was looking for someone. Silent until they reached the hotel, he turned to her and said: "What you and your father did today, along with the others, was a mighty fine thing. I'll never forget it."

She thought she saw some of the hardness leave his face and impulsively she wanted to comfort him, although she hardly knew how to go about it. However, she sensed in her quick way, that this immovable man wanted to talk about his friend, so she drew him to a chair in one corner of the verandah.

"The little we did," she said, "was the least anyone would have done."

"That's it," declared Durand, bitterness marking his tones. "More people here might have wanted to come to Larry's funeral, but they were afraid. Others didn't care. They didn't care that a good man was murdered . . . shot in the back . . . out in the hills. Larry Cramer was the best friend I had. He saved my life in Abilene once when a drunken, fool cowboy tried to shoot me in the back. And I guess I did the same for him somewhere back along the line. If he'd been killed in a stand-up fight, his loss would have been just as great. But this way, it was worse . . . plain murder, shot from behind like a dog."

Durand paused and his voice softened. "You saved me from the same end. I was lucky . . . he wasn't. He always was a hard luck man."

There was something else he wanted to tell her and she waited. "You see," he said, "Larry was a deputy U.S. marshal. He came here to spot a horse-stealing gang operating around Red Cloud. I was to meet him here and we'd work together."

"Then you're a marshal, too?" she asked.

He nodded and she said: "And I thought you were a drifter that first day. What will you do now?"

Durand looked straight into her gray eyes. "It's pretty plain, I guess. I'll stay here till I find out who killed him. Then I'll settle the score or they'll settle me."

Again she read the terrible, intense light in his face. She looked away, shuddering for him. When she looked at him again, his eyes were upon her and the piercing light had softened, lurking only in the depths.

Suddenly she said: "About yourself. You're one man against many. It's the same old story, Father says. One man is fast with a gun. He goes along until he meets someone faster. You'll be taking terrible chances."

He smiled brokenly, his face hardening, and she knew there would be no changing him. At dusk she saw him stride off down the street, a restless, driving man, moved by something he could not control. She went inside the hotel, feeling lonely and depressed.

Luke Givins sat on his front porch, smoking. Durand sat down and Givins studied him a while before he said: "You're restless tonight, which is only natural. My advice, such as it is an' being from an old man, is not to rush into anything like a wild bull. There's plenty of time. Don't run off half cocked."

Durand said: "I can't wait too long. Might set myself up for another ambush. That's the way they operate. From now on, I want to do the leading. Then I'll know when to open the ball."

"It'll open soon enough," Givins cautioned. "The thing is to know where you stand when you do open it. An' don't let Braden fool you. He's mighty smooth in many ways. Acts almost like a white man at times. Never does any of the killin' outright. In fact, best as anybody knows, he's never killed a man in Red Cloud . . . that is directly. But he's hard as steel. Some ugly stories have followed him here out of western Kansas. I've heard men say he's swifter with a gun than Kane. If he is, he's one helluva gun slinger an' next to lightnin'. The way I figure it, Kane kills for the pure love of it, while Braden just kills when he has to. When you bumped into him out in the hills, Braden must've figured there'd be no profit in jumpin' you there, though, as you said, Kane was ready to sling his Colt. That shows Braden's the smart one . . . the boss. The others think with their guns."

"Larry Cramer wasn't all I found in the hills," Durand

said thoughtfully. "At least one of the men who tried to get me was in on killing Larry."

Luke Givins sat up with interest. "That wouldn't surprise me none. But how do you know that?"

"One horse track was easy to follow. The left forehoof turned out at an odd angle, like the horse had been crippled when he was a colt. I finally lost the track where a herd crossed, but I picked it up close to where I found Larry in the brush. You know horses. Look out for that track. Maybe that horse will be coming through your barn one of these days. And there's something else, Luke, I'm a U.S. marshal. Larry was my chief deputy. We were after stolen horses. Which is another reason why horse tracks interest me."

Givins whistled softly with surprise, and, as Durand got up to leave, he said: "Watch the shadows. Some of Braden's men are in town tonight."

Chapter Five

Night had spread its dark blanket when Walt Durand moved up the street. Men stood or walked in the shadows. The saloons were waking up. Through board walls, he heard a woman's high, worn voice singing to battered piano accompaniment. He walked leisurely, watching the men. In front of the noisy Osage Girl he stopped. Cowmen lounged in front, and in the light from the swinging batwing doors he thought he recognized a familiar face. As he paused, desultory talk among the men suddenly shut off. And then a man swaggered forward, his hawk-like face framed in the yellow shaft of light.

As the man came forward, Durand felt a strange fury heat him. He waited. Now Smoke Crawford came closer and halted. Each seemed to wait for the other to move. Then Durand, low-voiced, said: "Found something out in the hills after I saw you. Thought you'd be interested. Guess you already know what I mean."

"How would I know," Crawford rasped back. "But I know you're too free with your talk . . . an' that's bad in Red Cloud."

"It all depends on how you back it up. I'm behind what I say. You can pass the word along to Kane and the big boss."

"You seem to want a quick finish." Crawford could not conceal his surprise at Durand's war-like talk.

With the old fury commanding him, Durand deliberately needled the man. "Just to prove this is no side show or idle talk, you can go for that gun on your hip when you're ready . . . if your nerve holds out."

Crawford's head snapped up slightly. He looked at Durand for a long, tense moment. His hand stiffened like a claw, but it did not plunge downward; instead, it hung there, hesitating.

"Go ahead, strong boy," Durand taunted. "They say you're hell with a gun . . . from the back." He wanted Crawford to reach for the gun, feared he wouldn't.

The little rider stood, silent and rigid, seemed to waver, muttered something, wheeled, and stalked into the saloon, his Mexican spurs tinkling with his rapid movement.

Durand watched the doors swing and finally stop. Aware of both disappointment and satisfaction, he walked away. He had almost forced Crawford to fight, and, although failing in that, he felt he had gained ground. From this point he had determined on an open fight, and he saw that he might have to do the early forcing. He had one booted foot on the first hotel step when he heard feet pounding and shouts. Immediately a man burst from the hotel, ran across the porch, leaped to a horse, and plunged westward down the darkened street. Durand went in to find an irate Cal Winston in the lobby.

"The damn sneak thief!" Winston roared, pacing and waving his arms. "He came in the back way, went up stairs, and pilfered some rooms. He ran like hell when he saw me."

Now Winston turned from Durand to Denton, the clerk. "Why in the hell didn't you stop that man, Denton?" Winston demanded. "There's a loaded six-shooter in that desk drawer. Use it! I put it there for just such emergencies."

"I'm no gunman," the clerk responded sullenly, his face red and angry.

Winston snorted with disgust, motioned to Durand to follow, and clumped noisily upstairs. Two doors stood open down the hall, one of them leading to Durand's room. With rising suspicion in his mind, he entered the room; it was in great disorder, his war bag open, its contents strewn on the floor, drawers in the scarred dresser pulled out, and the mattress flung half over. All of his belongings had been gone over thoroughly.

"Now what the hell!" Winston exclaimed, swinging around.

Durand finished his rapid inspection of the room. "Whatever he wanted, he failed to find. Nothing missing."

You didn't leave any money or valuables?"

Durand shook his head. "Maybe he wasn't after money."

"I don't like this," Winston said suspiciously. "Don't look like an ordinary thievin' job. Could be that fellow was huntin' you. Ever think of that? That's how it looks to me. You know, a sleeping man's an easy target . . . hard to miss. Many a man has died around a campfire . . . and I reckon some have been killed in beds in hotels. I saw this man come down the hall just as I came up the stairs. Denton said he sneaked in from the back. He brushed past me, went down the stairs, and out like a bullet. I believe you'd better swap rooms tonight."

They went downstairs where Ellen Winston stood waiting for them. "What's the matter?" she asked.

"Not a thing." Her father laughed. "Some wild cowboy just got in the wrong pew. He coyoted out when he saw me."

The explanation failed to satisfy her completely and she laid a questioning glance upon Durand.

"That's right," he agreed, at the same time noting that she was dressed as if for a visitor and he instantly thought of Matt Braden. She caught his studied look and left him with her father.

"She knows when I'm about half lying," Winston said sagely. "I can't fool her a-tall. Just like her mother," he said with pride.

Later, Durand took a seat on the porch deep in the shadows where he could view the street. Cal Winston's interpretation of the unknown rider's actions struck him as being peculiarly correct. Why had the man entered his room unless it was too kill him or to make sure that he was an officer? The first theory seemed to hold together better than the second, for the mere presence of a lone marshal was not considered a great worry in many parts of Kansas, especially among border haunts near the Territory with its timbered hide-outs.

Suddenly, as he sat there smoking, he glimpsed a man crossing the street to the hotel. The man came swiftly up to the porch, stepped forward noiselessly, and looked around with the quickness of a cat. He had started through the doorway when Durand called out softly: "Over here, Luke."

Givins's short-statured body came into the shadows and Durand rose to meet him.

"Got important news for you," Givins said in a subdued voice. "Where can we talk?"

"Right here."

"I found that hoss print!" The words came in a quick torrent, lighted by excitement. "After you left, I got to thinkin' about the hosses I had in the barn. I went down there an' checked every stall, looked at every hoss with a lantern. . . . An' reckon what I found?" He paused significantly and went on: "Well, it fits Smoke Crawford's mount. He's ridin' a big, square-built blue roan. The left forehoof turns out at a funny angle, just like you described it. I've seen that hoss a dozen times, I guess, but never noticed it before. Now that shore links up Braden's outfit, don't it? But it's no surprise to me."

"That gives us something to work on, Luke," Durand said warmly. "I'd like to know what Larry found out before they got him. He was on to something or they wouldn't have got him so fast."

"It's clear enough to me," Givins said crisply. "There's only one suggestion I'd like to make. Why don't you call in help from somewhere an' clean this bunch out in grand style?

Way it is now, you're buckin' a one-sided game . . . one man against a whole gang. I'll do what I can, but I ain't pulled a trigger since I played shotgun guard on a stage out of Denver. An' that wasn't yesterday. You have to shoot mighty straight an' fast if you want to come out of this standin' up."

Durand stood silently and thoughtfully, weighing the discovery about Crawford's horse. "There's not a reliable officer within a hundred miles of here," he said at length. "Besides, this is a sort of personal matter now. If that had been me, instead of Larry, he'd have figured it the same way. He'd have stayed here and fought it to the finish. And that's exactly what I plan to do."

Givins shook his head. "I'm not doubtin' your nerve. But you're being plain foolhardy."

"You're about right at that, I guess, but it's got to be done some way. I made my first move tonight." And then Durand told Givins about his brush with Crawford in front of the Osage Girl.

"An' Crawford backed down! Didn't pull a gun!"

"He wouldn't match this time. He wasn't ready and he was caught off guard."

"That's it!" Givins exclaimed. "He'll come at you when he has the edge, when the game is to his advantage. Oh, he's fast with a gun an' dangerous in a straight, showdown fight, I know. But don't ever show him your back."

"Not if I can help it."

The liveryman was still enjoying the word of Crawford's backing down.

"Well, well," he said, almost whispering, "Smoke Crawford, the lightning-rod boy, wouldn't face you. Walt, you're the first man that ever outbluffed that little gun-toter."

Presently Givins glided back they way he had come. His short, wiry figure soon mingled with the shadows and disappeared. His message left Durand with a new desire for action, mingled with elation. It was Crawford, and Crawford was Braden's man. If he had known about the horse when he met Crawford in front of the saloon, he'd have baited the man further, literally forced him to draw or shot him down. There was time left to find him again tonight.

Durand strode from the porch, shifting his gun belt as he hit the street. Red Cloud boasted six saloons and the Osage Girl was the largest. He checked two without finding his man, went on to the Osage Girl. Inside, men watched him a bit curiously tonight, and Durand guessed that word had gotten around about him. He had one drink, failed to find Crawford, and left to look through the remaining saloons. In a short time, he had covered all the hang-outs, but Crawford had vanished. To make sure, he walked to the stable.

"Now that's funny that he ain't in the saloons," Luke Givins told him. "That odd-footed hoss of his is still here. What're you aimin' to do?"

"Keep checking the saloons. He'll pop up later tonight, and, when I find him, he'll do some talking."

It was well after dark when Matt Braden rode impatiently into Red Cloud. He was late for his meeting at the hotel with Ellen Winston. Later tonight, he was scheduled to meet Red Kane at the Osage Girl for poker and drinks. In recent months, he had managed to see Ellen at least once a week, sometimes twice, and tonight he planned to reach a showdown with her. He had dressed carefully for the occasion—new high-heeled, hand-tooled boots, soft white, high-crowned hat, and blue silk shirt with a white scarf. In all the finery, his powerful body fit smoothly. He tied his horse in front of the raucous Osage Girl where, if he was interested, his foreman could see that his boss was in town. Except for the clerk, he found the hotel empty. He crossed confidently to the desk. "Well?" he asked quietly.

Denton threw frightened eyes at the man who towered before him in his colorful finery. "Red," he said nervously, "sent some drunk in here tonight after your man, Matt, but he missed the deal. Came too early in the first place and the old man caught him upstairs."

Braden cursed softly. "The damned fool! Did he get away?"

"Sure, but Winston gave me hell for not trying to stop him. It looked out of the way when I didn't make a move."

Braden's thick fingers drummed a tattoo on the desk. "By God," he said savagely, "Red's playing it out in the open too much. Someday he'll blunder in where I can't get him out."

Denton's eyes telegraphed a quick warning, and Braden, his manner changing swiftly, turned to see Ellen Winston entering the lobby. With a touch of the cavalier gracing his actions, he swept off his white sombrero and advanced to meet her.

He looked down at her, smiled, and said: "I've come for my answer tonight, Ellen."

She searched his face, saw the set jaw, the penetrating eyes, and confident manner. "You're a determined man, Matt," she admitted. "You don't give a woman much room to maneuver, do you?" Her low, soft laugh relaxed the stern set of his face and he was forced to smile.

She led him out on the porch and they stood looking out upon the darkened, silent scene of the street.

Braden said: "I'm a pretty patient man, Ellen, but I don't want to wait any longer. You've said yes and no long enough."

She laughed. "You can't expect a woman to say yes immediately. Give her time."

"I know, I know," he said easily. "But I'm a man who can't let a woman twist him, maybe fool him. I tell you I can't wait forever. I want you to give me an answer tonight."

One of his big hands gripped her arm and she felt his ponderous strength and she became aware of the swift current of his passions, his driving, surging, untrammeled spirit. He stood near her now in all his boundless strength, and, for the first time, she felt a quiver of fear seep into her.

And suddenly his arms closed around her and he started to crush her to him. "Why don't you tell me tonight?" he murmured, his face close to hers.

"No, Matt, no." Her arms stiffened, holding him off. For a moment, she thought he was going to force her against him, but at last his arms eased and he stood back slowly, as though he could not believe that she had refused him.

"You aren't used to people . . . especially women . . . saying no to you, are you?" she said huskily, breathing deeply.

His deep voice rumbled into a quick laugh, and as quickly his manner changed. "I've always had to fight for what I got," he said deliberately. "And it hasn't been easy. It's fight or go down these days. A man fights and wins until he meets a better one. Maybe a man who's a split second faster with a gun or just plain lucky. As for the women, you're the first one I ever wanted to marry. I haven't had time for many of them."

Boots broke in hollowly on the steps. Braden whirled alertly, suspicious of the noise and irritated by the interruption. A man called out in a hurried tone: "Matt?"

At the sound of the man's voice, Braden's tenseness vanished and reluctantly he crossed to the steps. "What is it this time, Red?"

"I want to talk to you."

"Can't it wait? You knew I'd meet you later. Why come up

here while I'm visiting Miss Winston?"

Almost in a whisper, Red Kane said: "This is important, Matt. I'll explain later."

"All right."

Braden went back to Ellen, who caught his ill humor at Kane's unscheduled visit.

"Think it over, Ellen," he said evenly. "I'll be back again and again . . . until you say the word, one way or the other."

Again she was conscious of his powerful person as he loomed over her, head bent looking at her, his body bulking broad and formidable. She marveled at his strength, not wholly in admiration, but with an unexplained feeling of fear.

Long after the two men had gone, she pondered Braden and the strange power that commanded him. In a way, it was akin to the unbending firmness and decision that drove Walt Durand when he stood on this same porch and talked about the death of his friend. However, as Durand would discuss in resolute tones plans to avenge the loss of a friend, Braden would talk money, cattle, land, and women. They formed the leading goals in his life, she decided, because they stood for something tangible, something to which he could apply his endless energy. It was like a game wherein he arrayed his greater, border-hardened strength against weaker men and always won. That is, as he said, until a man faster with a gun came along.

It was past midnight, as she lay awake in her room, that she heard the sound of shots down the street toward the saloons. She thought nothing of it as gunshots were not unusual at any hour in Red Cloud.

Durand stood patiently in the blackness cast from the mercantile store across from the Osage Girl, the glow of his cigarette a pinpoint in the shadows. He had patrolled all the saloons a second time without flushing Crawford and he had decided to wait it out here. The man had to show up somewhere, and his horse was still at the barn. *This time,* Durand thought, *I won't let him saunter out of trouble and into a saloon for protection.* A patience stemming from long hours in other tough cow towns like this one, waiting for some gunman to show himself, or for a horse to gallop in the night, kept his gaze roving the street where the saloon doors cast out their filtered corridors of light. It was near midnight and the street showed no life save for the stamping of horses that had been standing long hours at the tie racks. Durand shifted his position to look up and down the street for movement and saw nothing again. Unhurriedly he paced across to the Osage Girl for another look. He found the crowd dwindling, leaving only the hardiest, but a lively poker game continued in the back part of the place and bartenders still plied their trade without rest.

But Crawford was not among the revelers. Looking over the long bar again, Durand noticed a rear door that opened into the black mouth of an alley. Without hesitating, he swung back out the front way, intending to cut back and prowl the alley behind the saloon. When he came to the first side street, he went to his left. Here it was blacker and he moved with caution to where the alley made its intersection with the street.

He stopped, close against a board wall, and scanned the alley. Light from the saloon's back door threw a faint shaft that helped dispel the shadows and revealed only a single horse tied to a low shed. But time meant nothing in this game of stalking and he clung to his shadow-shielded post, waiting and watching. For a long time he stood there, waiting until he finally grew restless with the feeling that Crawford was not coming.

As Durand started back to Main Street, the night was shattered by the roar of two quick explosions, and down the side street past the alley he saw the flash and heard the blast of another shot. He half crouched against the board wall and, keeping close to the buildings, half ran in the direction where he had seen flame leap from a gun.

Chapter Six

A man's throaty cry of distress sent Durand plunging ahead in full stride, his gun drawn, eyes trying to pierce the gloom. Guns boomed again and wild lead smashed into the wall behind him. Durand was thinking fast, and the memory of other scenes came rushing over him, scenes at Abilene and Caldwell, where men fought and died in the dark, their guns showing flaming red. It occurred to him swiftly that he was a fool to interfere in a chance street brawl. But there was that compelling cry of a man in trouble, and instinct, together with his long training, prodded him on. Like a swift shadow he ran. Now a gun sounded ahead of him to his right and the shooting instantly broke out into a full-fledged battle. Durand halted, and, as he bent lower to better his vision, he saw outlined a man crouching with his back to a building, flame spouting from his guns as he fired down the street and to Durand's right. Then the crouching man's guns ceased as if he had emptied them and was reloading. At the same instant, the marksman on the right opened up again and the man in the street dropped flat. Durand heard boots pounding the hard earth toward the fallen man, and he began firing, deliberately shooting high. A high yell and the rapid passage of the man running down the narrow street to join his bunch was Durand's answer. He ran forward and the fallen man rose to his feet and whirled, facing him.

"Hold on!" Durand cried, pulling the man back and against a shaky board wall for protection. Both men were breathing hard as they waited, but the guns down the street were silent.

"Let's get out of here where a man can see what's comin' at him," the man said finally in a drawling voice. "My guns are empty. When that last fellow came up, I just flopped down and waited for him with my knife. Like a damned fool I took a short cut to the hoss barn an' three night owls tried to bushwhack me. Guess they figured I carried a payroll."

When they reached Main Street, the man insisted they stop at the first saloon for a drink. Durand accepted, more for curiosity and a closer look at the fighting stranger, and they entered the Silver Dollar, a lesser establishment nearest Givins's barn. In the bright lantern lights overhanging the bar, Durand saw a big-boned man with blue, friendly eyes, blond hair, face the color of saddle leather, and a laughing, reckless mouth. After one quick drink, they headed for the stable.

Suddenly the blond man said: "Hell, my name's Jim Wyatt . . . from Texas. Guess you wondered." He laughed a rich, booming, reckless laugh that Durand found pleasant.

"You hadn't offered it and I didn't ask it," Durand replied, giving his own name.

That stirred another appreciative laugh and Wyatt drawled: "Well, it might've been the late Jim Wyatt if you hadn't been curious and achin' to join a gun battle."

They walked on a while and Wyatt, as if thinking aloud, mumbled: "Durand . . . Durand . . . that's familiar somewhere to me." And in sudden inspiration he asked: "Ever been around Abilene?"

"You bet. Why?" Durand did not think it likely, because the man's face was not familiar, but if he had met Wyatt in Abilene with results harsh on the other. . . .

"Hell, you're Walt Durand!" the Texan exclaimed. "One night I saw you and an officer they called Cramer fight it out with five peelers. Prettiest shootin' I ever saw. Right out in the open street, with the show over in twenty seconds. Remember?"

"I remember," Durand agreed. Yes, there had been two against five, he and Larry Cramer, and within a few seconds, out there in the open street in the half light of dusk, he and Larry had knocked down three men, with the others fleeing.

Durand failed to elaborate on the gun battle and Wyatt shifted back to tonight's scrape. He told Durand he was moving a Texas-owned herd from the Territory to market at Elgin; how he had come to Red Cloud for supplies when the attempt was made to take his outfit's payroll.

"I knew this was a fast town," the Texan said with the reverence of a man who likes a good fight, "but not that fast the first night. They must have spotted me in a saloon earlier. From now on I carry a full cartridge belt, mister . . . and no payrolls."

Two of Wyatt's cowpunchers were waiting for him at the stable. He sent the payroll with them back to camp and called to Durand: "I want to buy you another drink and ask some questions!"

"We'd better do our talking here, instead of in a saloon," Durand cautioned. "The Osage Girl, for example, is a good place to talk and have it reach the wrong men."

Wyatt agreed with a nod. "I ought to know that by now."

"That where you were earlier?"

"Yes."

They were standing in Givins's little lantern-lighted office and Durand studied the Texan closely, saw his hesitation as he looked questioningly at Givins.

"He's one of the best," Durand assured him. "Go ahead."

"Well," Wyatt began, "it's hosses. Everybody has hoss trouble, it seems, but I've lost a whole remuda. Happened south of Red River. Cleaned them out slick as a whistle one night, crossed the river, and moved fast this way. The trail got cold on us after we crossed the Arkansas, comin' into the

Osage nation." Here his eyes brightened with interest, his long jaw hardened. "But not so cold we couldn't see they brought the remuda through this country," he declared, gesturing with his brown cigarette.

Durand said: "You're not the first man who's traced stolen horses to this section of the country."

"Looks like a big ring," Wyatt said. "The way it shapes up to me they must have one of their hoss hide-outs handy off in the hills north of here. There they can hold stock, feed and rest it during the day, and move it at night. Works pretty slick in a wild country, though it takes a lot of hands." Wyatt looked sharply at Durand. "Will you help me?"

Durand grinned. "It's the other way 'round, will you help me? I'm here on the same job, Wyatt."

"Maybe we both need help."

When Durand described events leading up to Larry Cramer's death, the Texan cursed eloquently and feelingly. Afterward, the three of them went to the Osage Girl. To Durand's surprise, the saloon had taken on added life at this late hour. With vague warnings rippling through him, he soon found the answer. Matt Braden, Red Kane, Cash Edmund, and several other cowpunchers stood at the long, polished bar. As the three men went up to the bar, Kane, his reddened eyes instantly hostile, looked at them with bitter amusement he made no attempt to conceal. At the same time, men along the bar, catching the unspoken exchange, ceased talking, and some began crossing over to the gaming tables for better and safer vantage points. That left the space between Durand and Kane open.

Watching Kane in the mirror, Durand had his drink and swung about, half facing the foreman. His dislike for the man struck him hard inside, made his face tighten and harden.

"Careful, Walt," Givins warned softly over his glass.

Behind him Durand felt the presence of Wyatt as the Texan also turned to watch Kane. There was the shuffling of boots as more men smelled trouble, and the silence was so keen Durand could hear a bartender nervously rubbing a glass with a towel behind the bar.

Then Kane's sneering voice cut through the silence: "Still playin' snooper?"

Durand's right hand moved with a swooping motion and Kane blinked into the cold mouth of a six-shooter. In three strides Durand closed the gap to the foreman. Behind Kane he saw Braden's dark eyes glittering, weighing his chances this way or that, Durand thought.

"Drop that gun belt to the floor," said Durand crisply. "I'm going to give you the chance to eat that word you like to use."

Kane's jaws jutted stubbornly; he made no move to unbuckle the gun belt.

"I'm not in the mood to wait too long for that belt to hit the floor, Red," Durand warned. "Drop it!"

Now Braden, scowling, demanded in an outraged voice, "What is this . . . a hold-up?"

Kane's big, meaty hands jerked once, settled back, and then reluctantly released the gun belt as Durand ignored Braden and took a step forward. Yet Kane was cool and he showed no fear. Glaring at Durand, he said sullenly: "You'd have a better chance with a gun, Marshal."

Durand motioned away from the bar and Kane came out swaggering, his broad, squat body poised and ready. Durand slipped his gun into its holster, unbuckled the belt, and handed it across to Wyatt. There was a confident smirk on the foreman's red face and he blustered to the attack as Durand squared off. Both men had tossed their hats to friends. Men who had left the saloon hurried back to watch a fight that offered no danger to themselves.

Glowering, with his head low, Kane came out, his arms close to his body. Durand waited for him, then slipped in, smashed him on the side of the head with a left jab and crossed with a right to the chunky man's mid-section. Kane stepped back, puffing, agony written across his sweating face for a moment.

"That's it!" Wyatt yelled. "Keep him away. Don't let him in close!"

But Kane had surprising speed. Angered and the right side of his face bleeding, he rushed Durand savagely, throwing a flurry of hammer-like blows; one of them smashed in Durand's chest and he felt himself giving ground as he tried to avoid another rush. Kane swarmed in, trying for the kill now, and Durand tied him up as they crashed against the bar in a wild, surging mêlée. Kane roared with rage as Durand's long arms prevented him from swinging and he fiercely threw his bullet-like head against Durand's chin. Even when the blow struck him glancingly, the impact jolted Durand into momentary blackness and he hugged and clinched the mus-cled foreman until his head cleared. Then, his strength flooding back, he cleared his right hand and smashed two heavy blows to Kane's red face. As the man sagged, Durand drove another fist up to the wrist in Kane's thick middle. Kane gasped suddenly, his face smeared with pain, but dog-gedly he covered up that vulnerable spot by crouching. Durand stepped back, watchful for another swift rush, but his opponent also sought time to catch his breath. And so the two stood there in the center of the yelling, wild-eyed circle of men: Kane swaying slightly, debating when to rush, Durand sucking in his wind, watching for an opening to put an end to this.

Through the noise of the crowd, Braden's voice reached

the fighters: "Cut him up, Red!"

Durand moved in, deliberately now on the balls of his feet, prepared if Kane rushed. But when the other hung back, his tired, bleary eyes wavering, Durand feinted with a long left hand and, as Kane moved sluggishly to meet it, followed swiftly with another smash to Kane's red-streaked face that knocked him off balance for a moment. And as the opening appeared along the belt line for an instant as Kane raised his arms, Durand threw his whole body behind a blow to the stomach. Kane wheezed and grunted in quick pain, flailed back weakly as Durand flung himself forward with all his weight behind his punches. The roar of the crowd filled Durand's ears as he rushed his hammering attack, sending Kane reeling against the bar. There was the open line along the midriff again. Durand moved for it, but, as he started to rip across his fist, Kane suddenly arched back against the bar and, using his arms and back for a spring, raised his sharp-heeled boots and lashed out like a kicking mule. With pain searing him inside, Durand was propelled backward and he wondered vaguely if he could get up from this. He landed at the rim of the circle, and, as he looked through haze-filled eyes, he saw Kane flying toward him, those sharp boot heels aimed for his face like two lances. Durand spun over and the boots struck the floor beside him. Both men staggered up at the same time. But the earlier punishment was still with the foreman, and he wavered, sagging as he moved toward Durand. And there it was again—the opening—and Durand threw his right to the broad target, and, through lights dancing before his eyes, he saw Kane wilt and flop to the floor like an axed steer. Durand stood over him.

Somebody said: "Bring a bucket of water. He's plumb out."

Wyatt and Givins were beside Durand as he buckled on

his gun belt with clumsy fingers. He sensed that trouble still lurked in the crowd, but in his exhaustion he didn't much care. There was a commotion as the water bucket arrived. At the first splash, Kane stirred, looking around dazedly like a caged wolf. Near him stood Braden, angered and contemptuous as he looked at his beaten top man.

Although beaten tonight, Kane's anger still blazed like a low-dying campfire, and in a harsh voice he prodded Edmund: "Get him with a gun, Cash."

Edmund shifted uneasily, hesitating, but he did not move his hands.

Durand called to Kane: "You satisfied now?"

The red-whiskered rider's mouth snared defiance. "Damn you, you'll hear from me again! An' I'll come shootin'! You jumped the wrong man tonight with your sneakin' fighter's tricks!"

"Where you hiding Crawford?"

"Crawford? Go get 'im if you want his meat."

"I'd do just that if I knew where he was hiding. Been hunting him all night. He's hiding in town because his horse is still at the stable."

Seeking an outlet for his anger, whetted by his beating before the crowd, Kane turned his wrath on Givins. "You're a damn' fine one, sidin' in with a bunch of strangers. I'll see that not another hand from our outfit puts a horse in your barn."

"I'll get along," Givins answered evenly.

"Leave him out of this," Durand warned. It was a shot in the dark, but, with Kane boiling mad, he decided to nettle the man further. He said softly, his voice hardly carrying to Kane: "You did a poor job in the alley tonight, Red."

Kane's swollen mouth opened slightly, but his eyes were wary. "More of your dirty talk, eh? What're you drivin' at?"

"You ought to know," Durand said dryly, and he saw that the subject had riled his man, that it had hit home.

"Shut up, Red," Braden cut in, and then the big man, the boss man, stepped from the crowd, waving his bungling foreman to silence. He crossed to Durand and eyed him critically, his wide, massive hands resting lightly on his hips near his guns. "All right," he said, "what do you want in Red Cloud?"

"What I want you wouldn't give up without a fight, so why ask for it?"

Braden's cold smile mirrored his answer. "Maybe you're right. That's good reasoning. I always fight for my rights. Ask any man."

"Trouble is," said Durand, "your rights don't include all you take in."

Braden bit back like a rasping saw: "Don't get too ambitious unless you want to back it up."

"I'll back it up. Try me."

"With what . . . talk?"

"No, this," and Durand patted his gun.

"All right," Braden said icily. "Only don't ask for quarter when you're whipped and howling. You won't get it!"

"I won't ask for it because I won't need to."

"We agree on that, then," Braden said mockingly.

The crowd gave away as Braden pivoted on his heels and called his men. As Durand watched, the outfit assembled and followed Braden outside to their horses. At the hitching rack, Braden looked backward once, then said to Edmund: "Tell Crawford to clear out. We'll ride slow and meet him at the cross trail."

Edmund shuttled a look back to the saloon, did not see Durand, and went down the street. Four doors down at a rooming house, he entered a narrow hallway and climbed upstairs. A knock on the door was answered by a low call. Crawford opened the door cautiously, came out of the darkness, asking: "What's up?"

"We're clearin' out. Boss' orders. You'd better high-tail it to the stable before that stranger gets there."

Like a cat, Crawford eased down the back entrance while Edmund reached the boardwalk in front. When he came back to the saloon front, the riders swung to their saddles.

Outside of town, they slowed to a trot. Kane rode in moody silence, feeling sore and swollen, with Braden beside him, the others trailing.

At length Braden said: "Red, I thought you had that Texan with the payroll spotted for an easy taking."

"Hell, we did!" the foremen flared. "Had him cornered till somebody busted in there. Guess it was the new man, because they came into the saloon together."

"You mean Durand?"

"Yeah."

"That's two empty throws you've made tonight."

Kane yanked his horse back so suddenly it reared. "Damn you, Matt," he snarled. "We do your dirty work, all of it! I handled that first snooper for you, an' I'll get Durand. But don't howl. If you don't like my style, handle it yourself and be damned."

"Ease off, Red, watch that crazy temper. Sure, you did a good job the first time. But we've got to be careful. For a bunch of reasons."

Kane's thick voice edged back: "That Winston gal wouldn't be one, would she?"

It was Braden's turn to give way to wrath. "Sometime, Red, you're goin' to talk too much in the wrong place! She figures in it, sure. When I get her, I'll settle down and live like a respectable cowman. But before I do, there's some jobs to be done, and you're the man to do them."

"Meanin' what?"

"That last horse herd. We'd better push them farther north where it's safer."

"Crawford says he wants no more of that. He's traveled between here and Red River so many times some of the men down the line are gettin' suspicious. Now he's afraid to take the next bunch north."

"You'll take them then."

"Not me . . . I got a chore to do here."

"Durand?"

"Sure. No man can beat me and live to tell it many times."

"He's your man?"

"I'll get him . . . front or back."

"That settles it. Just keep me out of it . . . and stay out of spots where I have to drag you out."

Kane laughed mockingly. "So you won't lose your respectable front, eh? It's got to be Mister Matt Braden, the cow king."

"If you want to put it that way, yes. But remember, I'm paying the wages for this flock of gun slingers you brought in. I've organized you into a successful outfit. Organization is something you didn't have before. And you may not have it long if you don't get your man, remember that."

"I'll get him."

Chapter Seven

Jim Wyatt's herd was passing south of town, kicking up dense columns of dust; cattle bawled as riders pushed eastward toward Elgin. Before he joined his outfit, the Texan told Durand in his earnest way: "You're right on top of a powder keg here. Don't set it off till I get back. Why, man, this town's mighty near as tough as Abilene and Dodge. An' there's two men you'd better watch . . . Braden and Kane. You had nerve when you challenged Kane and beat him in front of his own men. That would rankle any man, make him itch to get you. Now he'll dog you for sure. So I say hold off till I get back in a few days."

"Crawford will talk when I flush him," Durand said. "He slipped away from us last night during the fracas. Luke said his horse was gone when he went back to the barn."

"Well, save him for later."

"It all depends. Maybe he won't keep. Meanwhile, I'm anxious to locate that bunch of horses you lost."

"Just don't stir up a hornet's nest without me," Wyatt asked.

Durand waited until dark. Then, striking north, he left town, leading the pack animal. After covering several miles he camped in a wooded draw, well concealed and off the main trail. Rolling in his blankets, he slept until early morning grayness began lighting the darkness, cooked breakfast over a brush fire, and headed north, riding parallel to the trail. As he rode steadily, aiming for that particular region where he had discovered heavy horse tracks on his previous prowl into Braden's domain, he recalled Wyatt's advice the night before about locating the horses. "Now if I was hidin' stolen

72

horses," the Texan had deliberated, "I'd pick out the wildest stretch of country I could find, bunch 'em in a cañon, and quit worryin'. That's where I'd look if I was on the losin' end of the game." It was sound reasoning and Durand headed northeast, into that trackless range of hills, brushy cañons, and prairie. He pitched in late afternoon, hiding himself among close-growing jack oaks so he could watch until dark.

Early the next day he picketed the pack horse in a narrow, tree-lined cañon, cut a wide circle, which he completed at sundown without finding tracks. Before daybreak he quit camp and moved ahead. By the time the sun reared up, he had halted again, and he watched from the rocky prow of a hill. Lying belly flat in the rocks and brush, he could sweep the surrounding country with his eyes. There was a great, enveloping stillness here, broken softly by the spasmodic rush of a hot wind.

During the late morning two riders emerged out of the north. They rode at a fast trot and came nearest Durand at a point less than 100 yards below him on the grass-rich valley floor. Neither man looked familiar at this distance, but Durand's interest became watchful and keen now, and the strain of lying for hours in one position vanished. Not that they were unusual-looking men. They appeared to be ordinary riders except they were armed to the teeth, including short, deadly carbines slung close to each saddle for instant use, and they rode with the wariness of manhunters. They sat their saddles with the all-seeing, stalking stealth of government Indian scouts Durand had seen in the Dakotas, with the practiced eyes of men who hunted men. As Durand read all these signs, he felt an inward warning and instinctively he pushed closer against the rocky ledge where he lay as the riders inspected the ridges with long, unhurried, studied appraisals. He followed them with a puzzled frown until they passed out of sight where the shallow valley curved to a creek. After that, he lay behind the rocks for several hours, his mind on the gunmen. When afternoon shadows cast their images, he eased from his look-out toward his horses, hidden behind the hill in a thick growth of timber.

Durand was down the hill, deep in the timber, when he heard a horse's whickering across the hills to his right. His animals were directly in front of him and he cursed when the pack horse promptly answered the call. The *clatter* of hoofs on rocks in the distance sent him running. But as he grabbed the picket rope, he saw the dark shapes of two horses being pushed hard through the timber. There was a high-pitched yell of discovery. A rifle boomed, its bullet singing through the trees over his head. And then Durand, seizing his carbine, turned from the frantic saddle horse, for it was too late to ride out of here now. He took his stand where the timber grew thickest, where the two riders, if they came in after him, would have to expose themselves as they crossed a pinpoint clearing.

Now the pounding of the horses through the scattered underbrush had stopped. The men had dismounted and Durand saw them advancing cautiously about 100 yards away. He threw a bullet at the nearest man, saw him jump back and dive behind a tree. Rifles began searching the woods about him. Durand fired sparingly, content to wait for a good target, but none showed immediately. At his back rose the rough hill, and to his left and right thick brush matted the timber's floor. He had ridden up from the creek to the base of the hill and he wondered where along there they had found his tracks. How to break this stalemate concerned him now, and, when a heavy crackling of rifle fire sent the pack horse plunging wildly through the trees and across the opening, Durand saw his chance and took it. Gambling on the horse's wild flight to draw attention from him, he crouched low in the brush and scrambled to his right. Running low, he took a dozen quick steps, expecting to hear the close whine of lead through the brush. But so far there was only the fading *crash* of the frightened pack horse. In a few more strides, Durand knew he was lost from sight to the riflemen until he chose to show himself.

The difficult, more dangerous part of his plan came up and he paused to make sure of his position. He stood up and peered carefully, but the timber and brush, thickest at this point, hid the gunmen from view. He worked ahead until he was sure he had gone far enough. Then he roved to his left, still keeping within the cover of the timber. Presently he sighted the opening through the trees. The killers should be straight ahead of him. He looked low in the underbrush. And then from behind a brush clump emerged a tall man. He seemed to spot Durand at the same instant. He half turned and Durand saw alarm and something akin to fear flash across the gunman's bearded face as he dropped his rifle and flung one futile arm backward for the faster gun at his hip. Durand's gun boomed twice, the bearded man's once, sending its bullet crashing upward through the treetops. The man fell like an emptied feed sack, all crumpled, with dull surprise written across his slack face. But the second killer? Durand stepped back, moving away, looking to both sides. From his right then a rifle *cracked* and he fell to the ground, holding his fire. He lay like that until the *hum* of insects became a distinct chorus in the stillness again, overriding all sounds. There was no movement up ahead that he could hear, and, finally, he got to his knees slowly, watching, then eased away, circling the place where he believed the man to be. After ten minutes of silent stalking, he came up from behind—but the woods were empty here. But farther toward the creek brush crackled, and, as Durand pivoted that way, a rider flailing a black horse sprang into the open for a few seconds and disappeared swiftly into the timber.

Durand stood there until all sounds died out, turned and went back to the fallen rifleman. He recognized a face he had seen among Braden's crew the night of his fight with Kane. He covered the gray face with its owner's hat and strode off through the timber where his saddle horse stood. His pack horse he recovered a mile north, trailing a broken halter rope. He camped west of the gun battle, watched his back trail until well past dark, and headed for Red Cloud the next morning for supplies. He had hit into the heart of Braden's country, had failed to find the horses or Braden's headquarters ranch, but he had learned the savage thoroughness with which the man guarded his holdings.

The rider's dust was a spreading, yellow-gray blanket from where Matt Braden stood on the high porch of his ranch headquarters. He turned his big body and shouted to the bunkhouse: "Come up here, Red!"

Inside the bunkhouse, Kane said with mock regret—"Just when I'm winnin'."—and slammed his cards down on the table. The foreman actually was in rare good humor, for he had been winning pot after pot. He got to his feet and conjectured: "Now what could be itchin' Matt this early."

"Mebbe he's plannin' another trip south for us," Crawford said testily from the other side of the table.

"Well, if he does, you'll go," Kane replied.

"I ain't so sure."

"Don't let the boss hear you flap that tongue of yours," the foreman warned and stepped outside.

Braden stood with big hands on hips, his favorite stance, and watched the incoming rider with a frown on his dark face.

"Who's this comin' in?" he asked Kane.

Kane studied the rider and horse thoughtfully. "That's Rip Nixon," he said. "Nobody can kill a horse like that but him. But he ain't due till tomorrow. He's supposed to watch the main trail below here with Tom East."

"Where's East?"

"You figure it out. It don't look good the way he's pushin' that hoss."

Nixon, headed for the corral, but, beyond the main ranch building, changed his course when he saw the men on the porch. He presented a stooped, weary figure as he spurred the lagging, lathered horse close to the steps. "East got his yesterday evenin'," he announced lamely, deep-set eyes roving from Braden to Kane.

"Get off and come up," Braden told him.

On the porch, Nixon recounted his story, warily watching the two bosses for their reaction. "We cut his tracks where he crossed Big Warrior Creek," he said. "Knew he was workin' north, all right, because Tom found tracks the day before but lost 'em. We came up behind a hill an' we thought we had him sacked up. But he was goin' for his horses. We opened up an' had to run for the brush. Figured we had him cornered sure. About thirty minutes later, this fellow comes up behind us, shoots it out with Tom. Wasn't anything for me to do but hightail it out of there an' come back later."

"Was it Durand?" Braden asked.

"Hell, yes! I'd know that tall *hombre* a mile away."

"Damn you, Nixon!" Kane suddenly roared accusingly. "Why didn't you follow orders? Instead of goin' in there half cocked, why didn't you wait for him to come to you, all set up!"

"It just didn't work out like that," Nixon said defensively, watching Kane closely now.

What Nixon had feared came like a riding storm. Kane's body moved swiftly. Nixon stepped back, long arms half raised. Then Kane's fists struck and there was the dull, meaty sound of bone against flesh. The tall rider's head flew back, his body bent backward, and he toppled down the rough porch steps, a sodden, beaten hulk.

Kane's deep chest labored as he glared down at Nixon, his red face flushed and set.

Braden sneered: "Helps keep your men loyal."

Kane's fury still stung him. He shouted to the bunkhouse, and two men came out. "Come up here and get Nixon!" he ordered in a roaring voice. "Throw water on him and give him a drink . . . he needs it."

As Nixon was carried off, Braden remarked dryly: "One of these days, Red, somebody will haul you somewhere . . . with your boots on. Now, better bring everybody in."

When Durand rode into town, Luke Givins told him Jim Wyatt hadn't returned from Elgin and Durand decided to wait out the evening for the Texan. Meanwhile, he bought supplies and went to the hotel, washed up, and came down to the dining room. Ellen Winston's gray eyes rested on him with surprise. She came over to his table and he said: "You're the best sight I've seen in days."

Later, they met on the porch and she said she was going to the dressmaker's at the edge of town. He saw that he could accept that as an invitation or just plain conversation. He took the first, stepped up beside her, and offered his arm. "This is my first pleasant duty in a long time," he murmured as they walked away. "I welcome it."

They went westward in the early evening softness, lighted by a dull glow in the west. By the time they arrived at the dressmaker's house, a squat, three-room structure surrounded by a picket fence, the evening had shifted into night and stars began making their overhead play and a wind pushed softly out of the southeast. Durand sat down on the porch steps to wait after Ellen went inside. All the hardness of the last few days, climaxed by the short, fierce fight in the timber, was being washed away now by this night and he thought of what lay before him when he rode north again with a feeling of loneliness, distaste, and foreboding. His job, as he saw it here, had unerringly drifted into the old familiar pattern of men, guns, and horses, and he supposed that it would always be like this for him until he met a man quicker with his wrist or until he quit, and he wouldn't quit, not now.

After a while, Ellen came out and they crossed the yard to the street. Both hesitated, and Durand said: "Let's walk out a bit. I promise full escort."

She took his arm and they strolled westward. There was a faint hint of early fall in the rush of the wind off the prairie, bringing with it wild pungent smells. They walked a way slowly, Durand keenly aware of the young woman beside him as he caught the faint perfume from her hair. Finally they paused atop a slight rise in the prairie and looked up at the now brilliant display. Red Cloud, with its stormy passions and hates, seemed far distant to Durand, but the stars were very near. It was a strange feeling for him and he found himself wondering at this mood. He found it difficult to speak; he groped for words, failed to find them. When he looked at her, he saw the pale light on her face, revealing its soft contours. Suddenly her face was close to his, she was in his arms and he bent his head swiftly and kissed her, and for an interminable time he seemed lost in her infinite sweetness, in the softness of her lips, in the warmth of her body against his. When he raised his head, she stepped back and he murmured: "As an escort I'm not reliable."

She said slowly: "I didn't say you weren't." He felt her hands on his arms. She said anxiously: "Walt, when will all this gunfighting end?"

"When I get the men who killed Larry."

"Oh, I know. You told me that but. . . ." She was silent, studying him. "What about Matt Braden?"

"He'll get the same treatment if he had a hand in it."

Mention of the man's name fired him, and the softness of the night was fading now, swept aside by old, resurgent memories, by the revival of duties he had ignored for a while tonight.

She said: "You say that with such terrible anger. You seem so sure, so determined. A while ago you were another person . . . entirely changed. Now . . . I don't know. You're a stranger again. I. . . ."

"I don't say Braden did it himself," he countered, thinking: *Is she trying to protect him?* "But he must've been indirectly responsible. That makes a man liable."

"What if he can't control his men? It's common talk he has rough men under him. Some of them have been on the dodge for years, they say. I mean riders like Kane and Crawford. Kane's a bully. Dad says you beat him up."

"You heard the story?"

"The whole town knew it the next day. You're something of a hero."

Durand laughed thinly. "'Hardly that. More like a fool. And don't think Braden can't control his outfit . . . he rules with an iron hand. Kane takes orders from him only."

"You think he's a part of all this then?"

"Yes."

"You seem so positive about him, so sure," she said, troubled, her voice rising.

"I've good reasons to feel that way. Crawford was in on

Larry's ambush. I know that for certain. Horse tracks proved that. The same tracks where I was ambushed and you rescued me. Tracks tell more than men sometimes. There's going to be a showdown, I know that. It's already started, I guess. Maybe I won't survive it, but its coming. Frankly I'll welcome it."

He had spoken with the familiar, immovable hardness, and she flared back: "You're a born trouble hunter!"

She flung the words at him and was moving away now. He stood unmoving, surprised and at loss. And then from far back in his mind rose the suspicion that her concern for Braden must be real, and he recalled the man's visit to the hotel, his possessive air. The thought was gone quickly, but it left its shadow of doubt and suspicion. Durand strode after her, caught up in a few strides. She walked straight ahead without speaking and he paced silently beside her. They went past the dressmaker's house, where their walk had begun so auspiciously, and came to the hotel. As they went up the steps and reached the doorway, Durand said heavily: "I don't dodge trouble . . . if that's what you mean."

In the filtered light he saw her face, not a face showing anger as he had expected, rather one strangely reflecting perplexity and hurt. He felt stiff and awkward. He said—"Good night."—and left the porch, his boots making a hollow beat on the boardwalk.

An hour later, his packs filled with purchases he had made that afternoon, he headed north, leaving the pack horse behind. He had decided not to wait for Jim Wyatt, and he would travel light.

Chapter Eight

Durand pushed into the timber-studded hills, traveling faster than on previous scouts, for the country was becoming familiar to him. He passed the area where the gunfight had occurred and struck north in the general direction where he believed Braden's hidden quarters lay. He had arrived at that conclusion after careful scouting sweeps, and in late afternoon, as he followed a narrow trail siding a wooded, rocky ridge, he heard shouts and the rumble of hoofs in the valley below him. Moving to a break in the timber, he spotted four horsemen driving several hundred head of cattle toward a break in the hills to the east. As the herd's course ran along the route he had set, he followed.

Almost immediately his interest quickened. This herd was being pushed faster than ordinarily; this was no shift to fresh range, no routine job. There was an urgency in the way the riders often turned in their saddles to look behind them, in the way they drove the stock, swinging ropes and crowding the animals forward. Once the herd entered the gap in the hills, however, the riders slowed down, as if they had reached safety. At the same time, two men rode down to the herd, apparently from a post overlooking the defile, and joined the herd riders. A short parley followed. In a few minutes, Durand saw them break up and start pushing the cattle forward again, and it was sundown before they eased up and bunched them for the night.

Durand's turn came now. When it grew dark and the herd riders' campfire made its bright mark, he left his horse in the timber and roved ahead. As he came close to the camp, a figure occasionally rose and bulked in the light, and he could hear the low-pitched murmur of voices. Brush grew thick at this point and he crawled until the voices became fairly distinct and the pleasant smell of tobacco mingled with wood smoke reached him. Men lounged in the shadows against their saddles, talking and smoking before they turned in for the night.

"It wasn't easy today," Durand heard a rider comment.

"Gettin' tougher every time," an older voice agreed.

"I expected to find a bunch tailin' us all the way back. An' they will one of these days," the first man said with strong conviction.

"Sure they will. These ranchers just ain't organized yet. There'll be hell to pay when they do. We'd have a free hand long as we wanted if we'd let these cowmen alone. But the boss says the hoss market's gettin' hard to meet and we got to branch out. Cow money's good, but stock's hard to wrangle . . . an' it'll get harder."

From far in the shadows a man said menacingly: "Your blood's just thin, that's all."

Durand thought he recognized the prodding, knife-edged voice of Cash Edmund.

"Don't get riled up," the older man soothed. "We're just talkin'."

"It's damn' poor talk if you ask me!"

"It's sensible talk if a man knows he might go over his head."

"You ain't over yet."

"No, an' I don't aim to!"

A taut silence hung over the campfire circle. Then a man got up, announced—"I'm turnin' in."—and went to his bedroll on the far side of the group. Others followed, their jumbled talking coming piecemeal to Durand, until only two men sat before the fire, which was burning low. They sat without speaking for what seemed an interminable time to the man in the brush; presently they stood up and drifted toward him, stopping at the edge of the brush rimming the campsite.

"I don't like Al's talk."

"His guts are runnin' low," snarled a voice. It was Cash Edmund, speaking in his contemptuous, bitter way.

"What's got into Al and Crawford?" the first man asked.

"That's easy to figure. It's tougher to get hosses through from Texas now, an' the boys don't like to handle Kansas cattle. 'Fraid they'll set in bad north of the Territory."

"Well, I can understand that."

"Yeah, but what the hell!"

"Where we takin' this bunch?"

"North, past the ranch."

They moved away and their voices faded out as Durand lost their dim figures among the trees on the far side. He waited until the fire's bright glow slackened and the camp lay long-shadowed and silent. Then he crawled back the way he had come. Finally, when he lay down in his blankets, he felt that he was on the verge of discovering something big. He had found a herd of stolen cattle, learned dissension stirred among Braden's men, but he was no nearer solving the riddle of the stolen horse ring.

Before sunup he was riding, and, when the herd started marching sluggishly north, he watched from the high point of a hill, content to follow at a distance. All morning, as he watched the herd travel faster than it wanted to, he knew that events were shaping to some sort of climax. On other scouts into the hills, he had been aware of a certain hopelessness as he searched for tracks and found nothing that helped. Today it was different. He might find something that would lead him to Larry Cramer's killers.

The day advanced to early afternoon under a blazing sky

and there was no halting for the tired herd. No new riders appeared, and, for the first time that day, Durand began to fear his hopes might prove groundless. When the low, curving line of a tree-bordered creek took shape ahead, the cattle hurried up for water. After about an hour, with the riders making no move to start the herd rolling again, Durand wondered at the delay. They couldn't dally here until dark if they hoped to pass the ranch, wherever it was. But after horsemen rode to the crest of a hill to look into the northwest, Durand figured they were waiting for someone. Was it Braden and Kane? From his post in timber, with his horse hidden in a draw, he could look straight into the little cluster of men lolling under the cottonwoods along the creek.

Finally a horseman broke down the look-out hill, and the men at the creek bestirred themselves. A short time later two riders loomed out of the northwest. They came at a ground-eating trot, passed the base of the hill in easy view of Durand, and rode straight for the creek where the crew waited.

There was no mistaking the new horsemen: Matt Braden's massive shoulders, Red Kane's bulky body, heavy in the saddle. Durand saw them dismount and merge with the men. There appeared to be an earnest parley going on, and then Braden and Kane went to their horses and rode off, back northwest, and the men left behind mounted and began routing the cattle from the creek bottom.

As Braden and Kane broke from the parley point at a gallop, Durand followed, a rising expectancy gripping him. He hovered at a close, dangerous distance for fear he might lose them in the broken reaches. They never looked back, riding steadily northwest. Just before sundown they swung into rougher country, broken by sharp, rocky hills and thick timber; it was country new to Durand, farther west than he had scouted.

Fred Grove

At the mouth of a narrow cañon passing through high limestone walls, Braden and Kane halted. Puzzled, Durand held back. They seemed to be waiting for something, for a signal, perhaps. Almost at the same time, a sombreroed man rose from behind a pile of rocks overlooking the cañon's entrance and waved them on with a flourish of his rifle. When Braden and his foreman pounded into the defile and disappeared around a bend, the rifleman sank down from sight, and Durand, shielded only by sparse tree cover about 100 yards away, swung back to avoid being spotted by the lookout. After picketing his horse, he eased back to watch the cañon and wait for darkness. Had he found the entrance to Braden's well-guarded hide-out? If he managed to slip past the first rifleman, would there be others stationed along the twisting course of the cañon? With gray eyes roving the rocky cañon wall where the guard lay concealed, Durand was struck by the organization of an outfit that drove stolen cattle boldly across country in daylight, that posted sentries on its domain, and, in general, operated with a military smoothness.

When the hills lay deeply shadowed, Durand squirmed to the edge of the timber; there, bending low, he crossed the opening to where the black mass of the limestone wall reared up. He stepped into the cañon, pressing against the wall, listening. Overhead where the rifleman lay, there was no sound. Durand breathed easier; he had not been seen. He went on, treading a well-beaten, twisting trail. There was a strong chance that other look-outs were posted atop the cañon walls or along the trail itself, he realized readily as he studied the narrow defile, fully aware of its dangerous angles. With straining eyes, he watched the formless blur of the rim and bends, and presently found what he was looking for—a side trail angling off up the steep wall to his right apparently to the sentry's post.

Standing at the foot of the trail, he debated whether to climb it to the top or wait a while. Now he picked up the pounding of a horse footing a rocky trail overhead. The pounding drew rapidly closer, and, as Durand pulled back into the deeper shadows, half sliding down the sheer trail came a horse and rider. In a rattle of rocks and clouds of thick, acrid dust, they reached the bottom of the trail, whirled north up the cañon, and blinked out of sight at a run. The outpost was going in for the night.

Darkness enveloped the cañon as Durand moved ahead, while overhead the stars made their early, scattered pattern, giving promise of a bright moon. The outpost's dust still hung in the still air, and twice Durand passed off-shooting trails. He ignored these, but unexpectedly the cañon walls widened and the timber suddenly petered out. And before him lights showed their yellow splash in the rich night, throwing into rough focus the vague outline of buildings and corrals. They appeared to lay in a great bowl-like depression arching out from the cañon's bottleneck. Nearest him loomed the main buildings, with the corrals beyond to the north. The vastness of the layout surprised him; even in the hazy light there was no mistaking the well-planned order of the buildings. Then Durand moved for the west wall, a tall, stalking figure who moved swiftly.

He paused within the shadows of the wall as a door slammed in the rear of the main ranch house and the brittle *clap* split the stillness. Fainter came men's voices from the corrals, and the pounding of a horse upon the hard valley footing. A southeast wind nudged into the bowl, moaning softly. Encompassed here within the towering walls, every sound seemed doubly clear and close. Ahead, Durand located the long shape of a low-slung, lighted bunkhouse, and it was from here the bulk of the noise carried. Past the bunkhouse loomed the ranch headquarters, a one-story building spread out low. He took up position between two sheds where he could view the front door of the bunkhouse and one side of the house's long porch.

Light from the bunkhouse threw long yellow fingers toward the house, and from within men's voices rose and fell, and Durand surmised that a game was in progress. Presently a man left the bunkhouse and went upon the porch of the big house, dimly alight in front, his boots sounding on the board steps. The game continued without a let-up, but, as if no longer controlled by a restraining hand, voices grew louder, quarrelsome, higher, and more insistent. There was a short silence, then a single, violent curse ripping out, the *crash* of a chair and the quick blast of a gun. A man's painful shout was heard; men fled out into the yard, stopping in a few strides to look back. As they milled for a moment, a heavy voice from the front porch of the big house checked them: "What in hell's goin' on down there?"

A man shuffled uneasily. "Jim winged the kid," he explained. "Been sore all evenin'. The kid was losin' heavy, claimed Jim marked the deck."

Now three men came down from the porch and entered the bunkhouse. Matt Braden's commanding voice sounded, whipping the men together as they carried the wounded man to the ranch house. Within a short time the place quieted down, men drifted silently back to the bunkhouse, and soon only three cowpunchers sat squatting near the door, smoking. When they turned in, and the bunkhouse darkened, Durand riveted his attention on the main building, which was still alight in front. For a long time he watched, until those lights went out and all movement ceased. He hesitated between going among the shadowy corrals and sheds. Somehow he felt there was more to be found here, yet he hardly knew how to go about it, and there was the constant danger that he would be cut off from his horse.

Durand's decision to stay came unexpectedly. As he peered north with the buildings, dark and silent, about him, the bell-tone clear neighing of a horse rang wildly across the bowl like a trumpet's blast to a cavalry troop. That decided him instantly, pulled him away from the sheds, back along the west wall, past the scattering of outer buildings until he detected the restless stamp of horses and saw the high shape of a big rail corral. To his right, within a rope's throw of the corral, rose a low shed. Here he stopped to inspect the corral. What he saw sent a quick ripple of excitement through him. In the light of a full moon he saw fully half 100 horses moving restlessly. And as he stepped closer to the rails, a great, massive black horse, stirring nervously, caught his eyes and dominated the scene. The magnificent animal turned suspiciously, threw up his big head, and wheeled back into the milling bunch. But not before Durand saw the LX brand on the wide, muscled shoulder.

The brand's discovery—Jim Wyatt's Texas brand—drew him against the rails, tense and alert. Not only had he found Matt Braden's mysterious headquarters, which Cal Winston said no Red Cloud cowpuncher had talked of seeing, but he had stumbled onto a stolen remuda. There probably were others, but this bunch was Wyatt's, and that was enough. His mind running eagerly over his chances of getting the horses out, Durand pivoted to observe the main building and bunkhouse—they were still dark. He could free the remuda from the corral easily enough, but he was afoot and the thunder of running horses would bring men pouring from the bunkhouse; if he did get them down the cañon now, they'd be scattered in the hills. Neither could he return to his horse, ride back to the corral, past the buildings, without arousing the camp.

The sound of voices somewhere behind him pulled Durand around, sent him crouching against the rails. Two men were ambling slowly toward the shed, talking in low undertones. In the stillness they seemed much nearer than they actually were. Durand pushed low against the rails, conscious of a real danger now. These men could cut him off from the only escape route down the twisting cañon. And what had drawn them out to the corral this time of night?

Durand waited and watched in the shadows, a Colt in his right hand. Scarcely twenty yards away, near the corral gate, the men stopped, their talk having ceased as they neared the horses. They stood clearly outlined in the soft light, two tall men who stood straight, looking suspiciously at the herd, which still stamped nervously. For a long time they seemed to stand there, eyes sweeping the shadows. Of concern to Durand was that they would pace around the corral. If they swung to their right, they would run straight into him where he crouched low against the rails. And so he waited, half expecting this and the one-way choice of being forced to shoot his way out.

But they did not move toward him. Instead, one of them muttered with evident irritation: "Don't see a thing wrong. Maybe a coyote's been prowlin'. Hosses don't like varmints. Looks quiet enough to me. I'm ready to go back to my bunk."

His companion wasn't so sure. "These hosses been restless all night," he rejoined. "Look at that big black stud. The way he moves. He runs the bunch. There's a hoss. I'd take him if Kane wouldn't raise hell. For some reason, Kane's mighty anxious about this bunch. When he heard that stallion's blast, he got up, told me to come out here in a hurry. Hell, you'd think somebody was skulkin' around here, the way he talks. He says we move the whole bunch this mornin' to the main corral in the hills. The boss don't like to use the home ranch for that kind of stuff, though how a man could get in here I don't know."

"We'd better turn in. Kane'll be up early callin' for a crew."

"Reckon so. Damn Kane, anyway, for routin' a man out at this hour. Let's go in." He paused for a last appraisal of the stallion and said admiringly: "That stud keeps 'em riled, don't he? There's a hoss!"

They turned back, still talking, and Durand felt the tension snap, as if a taut wire had been snipped. He waited until they dissolved into the gloom as they walked for the bunkhouse. He did not hesitate now, but strode toward the cañon. Bigger game lay ahead. He would tail the horses to the main corral when the crew started them out in the morning. In open country he could make the break he dared not attempt here, boxed up in a cañon's dead-end. He moved past the big house, which was still without light, and reached the point where he had left the thin timber to scout the layout. Looking back, he saw the buildings were still dark. One shot, he thought grimly, and the place would be alive with fighting men.

It was as he started to enter the timber that the first warning, vague as it was, touched him like the sharp point of a Sioux lance. Somewhere, here in this shadowed, depthless dimness, a danger lurked, and he stopped, motionless. The cañon trail lay like a dull bed of silver from light straggling through the trees. No movement on the trail, he decided. Another step. He whirled to one side, stiffening. Directly before him a man moved like a wraith. . . .

Chapter Nine

The man had come out of nowhere, it seemed, from the timber beside the trail. In a swirling blur of action, Durand caught the flash of something descending upon him as he tried to step aside. As he did so, metal ripped high into his left shoulder. He swung with his right hand, with the short, weighty punch of a barroom fighter, and felt pain shoot into his knuckles. The man was down from a blow to the head, and now both struggled for the knife. His assailant's quick, hard breathing sounded like a bellows; his body was wiry and lean and he fought with a silent stubbornness of unexpected strength. Neither could draw a gun in the close mêlée, but finally Durand's fingers closed upon the knife hand, and quickly he had the knife. At length, when he staggered up, the lean man lay, still and grotesque, in the trail, and Durand felt a wave of sickness engulf him as he stared down. The fool! He could not be positive in the gloom, but he thought he had seen the man with Braden's crew the night he whipped Kane in the saloon. Probably another sentry prowling the trail who had posted himself here after Durand had come up the cañon to the ranch. It didn't matter what the man was now, he thought, except he was lucky not a shot had been fired to awaken the sleeping gunmen behind him. Durand dragged the burden well back away from the trail, leaving it behind a pile of rocks. The missing man would doubtless be discovered later, but not until after the horses were moved out. Durand was counting on the crew, in the rush of an early-morning drive, being too busy to launch a search for a missing member until later.

Weariness smote him as he left the place and went down the night-silvered cañon trail. The fight had been forced

upon him, but he could not entirely erase the ugly feeling of
having killed a man. Yet if he were the man behind the rock
pile, he thought grimly, there would be no regrets. Past the
mouth of the cañon he went, taking no chances if the outpost
had returned. Beyond, in the timber, he found water where
he washed his shoulder. He was lucky. He could move the
shoulder without too much difficulty. Moving the horse to
another picket, he threw down his blankets. One swift
thought of Ellen Winston came rushing over him before he
fell asleep.

When gray dawn spilled over the hills, he was up and scanning the cañon trail. An hour later, the growling rumble of
hoofs came from upcañon. The crew was moving the stolen
horses. The rumble heightened into a steady drumming that
shook the ground, and then out of the defile came a lead rider
with horses led by the black stallion close bunched behind
him. They swept westward, following a low break in the hills.
Durand, from a close-in timbered knoll, counted four men
riding after the remuda. He mounted and was forced to set a
fast pace, as the horses were traveling at a rapid clip with the
stallion following the lead rider.

They clung to the hill trail for several hours, then swung
across a long open stretch of gently dipping prairie, only to
cut a course southwest back into the hills. Travel was
slower here and the remuda tired. As Durand watched, the
lead rider slowed and the crew began bunching the horses,
holding a wide circle. After that, one man rode ahead, disappeared into the timber. After several minutes, he
pounded back. As if his return were a signal, the other
riders started the horses moving again, and shortly a wide,
wooded ravine appeared into which the lead horseman
headed without hesitation. With a quick surge of pounding
hoofs kicking up dust, the remuda and riders followed,

swallowed up quickly in the cleft.

Earlier, Durand had been forced into reluctant admiration at the swiftness and facility with which the men handled the half-wild horses. Now, impressed at the completeness of this hide-out, he dismounted and carefully hid his horse. Somewhere in this gorge-like slash in the hills lay the main corral, cleverly hidden and difficult to approach. A man could ride within fifty yards of its entrance and never give it a second glance.

Around noon, a thin column of smoke spiraled lazily above the ravine, hanging slowly in the windless sky. Not long afterward, the four riders who had driven in the Wyatt horses emerged and proceeded back at an easy trot on their old course. It took Durand, afoot, some time to work himself into position on the east side of the ravine where he could look down and see what lay below. At first glance the view was disappointing. The place was well masked, even from this point. But at the north end now he saw a glistening big water hole and rich grass that lay like a green blanket in scattered openings where the trees grew thinly. Bisecting the ravine ran a high, stout rail fence, which cut off about three-quarters of the wooded area, and behind this, to the north, horses grazed in small bands. Where were the guards? From here the entrance was obscured by an outjutting shoulder of rock and timber. Durand got his answer soon enough.

Below him a man strode from a cabin half hidden by overhanging rock. Then a second and a third man appeared. Carrying a bucket, the first man went through a crude gate at the fence and paced down to the water hole. The others hung back in front of the cabin. After a time, the man with the bucket came back, and the three either sat or walked restlessly near their quarters, although never far from three rifles propped against the cabin's wall. Apparently these men,

Durand judged, made up the entire force guarding the stolen horses. An opportunity was presenting itself. If the guards stayed bunched like this, he might break the horses from the corral, knock down any man who tried to stop him, and start the herd for Red Cloud. The longer he considered it, the stronger the plan appealed to him. Last night's inaction while nosing around Braden's ranch, discovering the horses, and being unable to do anything about it, rubbed him like a raw rope burn. Although it was three against one here, those were the most favorable odds he had encountered lately. A plan took shape in a rush, and he shifted about to put it in operation. The surest way, as he sized it up, was to ease down the steep wall behind the cabin and go for the men, instead of the horses.

As Durand rose to his knees to begin the descent, a guard rose from his place in front of the cabin and stared off across the ravine. Another guard's head jerked up suspiciously. What pulled their eyes that way? Durand hesitated, waiting. Almost simultaneously the three grabbed their rifles, and a shot shook the cleft. Durand stepped back, puzzled. Was this some rancher who had trailed his stolen horses to the corral? While he waited for the action to unfold and point its course, the guards scrambled into the cabin and began trading shots with the hidden foe across the ravine. For a short, roaring spell, both sides swapped lead. From his post above the cabin, Durand was still unable to locate the attackers, who did not seem to be in strong force, judging by the shots. As yet he has seen no movement, and it occurred to him they might be moving to positions overlooking the ravine.

The duel dragged on with the guards clinging to their cabin fortress, while the opposing riflemen threw only an infrequent slug, enough to keep the trio bottled up inside. Now the purpose behind this seemingly faint-hearted plan of attack changed with the sudden movement of men spilling through the timber south from the cabin. Obviously they had found the well-concealed ravine mouth and, unnoticed, were going to take the cabin from the rear if possible. Durand glimpsed heavily armed, big-hatted, raw-boned men, edging closer to the cabin, and he lay flat to watch the climax of this strange battle.

One man made a rush for the cabin's rear, hidden from the ravine's rim by the overhanging rock. There followed the *crash* of a door being kicked open, a fast, thunderous blast of Colts at close range. Suddenly a man broke from the front of the cabin, running like a wild horse. And on his heels from the cabin, with two smoking colts in his hands, burst a familiar figure—Jim Wyatt, the Texan. Wyatt yelled to the fleeing man to stop. The warning went unheeded. One of the Colts belched flame. The man staggered, dropped to one knee, lurched up, tried to run, and then whirled like a wolf at bay, presenting the grim, tense picture of a cornered fighting man willing to run his luck to the string's short end. A Colt flickered in his swift-moving right hand. Guns *boomed* almost as one. The guard flopped back, his gun falling from his hand. Wyatt approached slowly to look him over. Inside the cabin, a hush had settled. As Wyatt turned and paced back, Durand rose and shouted down to the Texan and his men. Rifles and Colts swung alertly to cover the rim. Wyatt's yell of recognition followed, and Durand began the steep descent, his sharp-heeled boots starting tiny avalanches of rock and earth. At the bottom, Wyatt, flanked by four men, waited.

"Durand! We cleaned out this bunch. But you?" Jim Wyatt could not conceal his amazement.

"Here on the same business," Durand explained. "I'll say you cleaned them out. Fastest gun work I ever saw. You took a chance going into that cabin. Any more men around here?"

96

"None we've seen," said Wyatt eagerly. "We was ready to move in and clean out this wolf's den when they came in with more hosses. We waited and four riders pulled out. That just about evened the odds."

"That last bunch of horses belongs to you," Durand said.

Wyatt's face held disbelief.

"That's right, Jim," said Durand, and outlined events from the time he had left Red Cloud leading up to the corral fight.

The Texan's broad smile widened. "Then you trailed 'em here with the idea of takin' the hosses back to Red Cloud?"

Durand nodded, and Wyatt said reproachfully: "You got too much nerve for your own good, Walt."

Durand laughed, remembering Wyatt's flying assault on the cabin. Another man joined the group, and Wyatt sent the men to cover the entire ravine. While he waited near the cabin with Durand, he said: "That trip to Elgin paid mighty well. We learned plenty. Ran into a young cowboy in a saloon. He'd been drinkin' heavy for a couple of days and was feelin' low. One of my boys took a likin' to him an' it seemed he was broke and homesick for north Texas. Come to find out this young fellow had worked for Braden's outfit. Sort of drifted in here and tied up with 'em as a bronc' rider. Well, before long he didn't like the brand of orders Kane gave out in his high-handed way. So he pulled out . . . in a hurry an' at night. But he'd been there long enough to know where this hoss hide-out is, an', when he found out my outfit hailed from Texas an' had our eyes open for hosses, why he told us everything he knew. Location of the corral, size of the usual horse guard. He didn't know about any LX hosses up here, but that was enough to send us back to Red Cloud in a hurry. You'd pulled out, nobody knew where, not even Miss Winston. But with what that lonesome Texas peeler told us, we found this place in pretty fast fashion. Spotted it late this mornin'. Like I said, the bunch was all set to ride in here and take it apart when this other bunch of hosses comes in. An' you say they're mine?"

Wyatt had been pacing slowly about as he recited his story, following the progress of his men as they covered the ravine and reappeared at intervals. Suddenly, like a clap of thunder, a Colt barked at the far end, then another and another, chased by a silence that hung menacingly over the ravine. None of Wyatt's men showed. Together, he and Durand went to the rail fence, studying the timber and rock-covered north end of the ravine from where the shots had sounded.

"Maybe we missed one," Wyatt ventured.

"He'll have to move fast to get past those boys of yours," said Durand. "But this thick brush makes easy cover. He might make it."

Durand's observation was borne out when Wyatt's force came walking to the fence presently, crestfallen and angry.

"Guess he got away, eh, Charlie?" Wyatt began.

Charlie Worth nodded in disgust, lean shoulders slumped, hands hooked in his in belt. He said: "That he did. Their north end look-out, I guess. I saw a man run for his hoss. I cut down on him, dusted his boots, but he went out of there like a Comanche, hangin' Indian-style on the off side of his hoss. That still didn't make sense because we'd scouted clear around the ravine, you remember. When we all got up there, we found a trail just wide enough for a skinny goat. He got out that way. But it was a good piece of ridin'," Charlie concluded.

Wyatt rubbed his stubbled chin and spat into the dust thoughtfully. "What do you make of it, Walt? Wonder why he hung out while the fight was goin' on?"

"Maybe he was cut off when the battle started. If he was

cool as the other men you met here today, guess he stuck around to see who found the hide-out. He'll make tracks now."

"In that case," Wyatt observed, "our friend Kane'll know about this in a few hours. When he hears it, he'll come a-smokin'."

"We'd best move these horses out of here where we can hold 'em. Which means Red Cloud. Take every animal you find, we can hold them all."

While the horses were being flushed from the vicinity of the water hole, Durand's gaze traveled to the black LX stallion, over his ebony coat rippling and glistening with muscles under the searing sun. Wyatt, catching the interest, asked: "What do you think of him?"

"Think of him? Most powerful horse I ever saw. Worth more than the whole bunch. It's little wonder you followed him from Texas."

"I'll give him to you," said Wyatt impulsively.

Durand, overwhelmed, said: "I don't want to take your best animal. That's too much."

"There's no argument now," said Wyatt decisively. "He's yours." And he rode off to help a rider cut a wild mare back into the herd.

The drive to Red Cloud began. While Wyatt and his men pushed the horses fast, stopping only for water, Durand acted as rear guard and scout. The only corral large enough to hold the plunging, kicking, squealing animals lay behind Luke Givins's stable, and Wyatt promptly posted cowpunchers to watch them that night and next day.

The second evening after reaching town, Wyatt sought out Durand at the stable, which served as a gathering place for the Texans.

"What's up?" asked Wyatt.

"I'm waiting."

"For Braden and Kane?"

"Guess that's it. One man got away to warn them. They'll be here . . . pretty sudden, I believe, after the horses. You think the same?"

"That's the way I figure it. They're too big an outfit to have men killed an' their stolen hoss den left bare without trying to get some of it back. 'Course, they'd rather get a shot at you than have the horses back. Three men will watch the corral tonight."

"Jim," said Durand, "you ought to be a marshal. You think of all the angles."

A little later Durand swung off down the street for a quick trip to the hotel. He wanted to know of any large batches of riders prowling the town and what went on along the seething saloon row. He had seen Ellen Winston only once since returning, that during the noon meal at the hotel. Tonight, despite the growing imminence of a showdown fight, thoughts of her trailed through his mind in steady succession. As he passed the hotel corner, a man moved in the shadows for the rear of the building. He would not ask after her tonight, Durand thought, as he stepped upon the porch. Cal Winston sat in his favorite battered chair in the lobby, and Durand spoke a low greeting and passed on to the desk. He was near the stairs when Ellen came from the dining room.

He spoke, the words coming slowly: "Hello, Ellen."

Her face was flushed, as if she had just come from the kitchen. Her gray eyes were bright and clear, certainly an appealing picture to him.

Durand started to move on, but she said reproachfully: "You're always in a hurry. Always on the move."

"It's because I have to be," he murmured.

"Sometimes I think it's because you want to."

"I don't make the choice."

She did not answer and he looked into the depths of her eyes and saw the coolness there—or was it bitterness? And, swiftly, the night she had walked away from him blazed again in his mind like a flaming torch in his memory. He said: "I haven't changed. I'm the same man."

"Nothing can change you?"

"Nothing, I guess."

After that, she was moving past him and he was going up the stairs, silently cursing the stubbornness that bound him to a code he could not break. At this moment, the trend of events before him, events his training and experience warned him were shaping toward a fierce showdown as certain as he lived, had never seemed more baffling and deadly. It left his self-confidence wavering, which was a new sensation for him.

In his room he tried to shake off the effects of his brief meeting with her. He stood looking out the window, seeing nothing, blaming himself for showing a dangerous weakness because of a woman. For that reason, in the manhunting trade, he had always endeavored to avoid women as a strong man avoids too much whiskey or poker. Until he came to Red Cloud, he had been successful, he told himself, but this was something he could not ignore and step past like the batwing doors of rowdy saloon.

With a start now, Durand realized that, in his abstraction, he had been standing before the window for perhaps several minutes, lost in thought. When he had come in, he had absently left the door open, lighted the lamp, and turned it low on the old bureau, and now, from out of the deep blackness shrouding the hallway, floated a subtle, yet keen, warning that stiffened him, turned his muscles hard and tight, sent little streams of sweat down his chest. Somewhere in the hall a board *squeaked* under a booted foot; a pistol shot would have sounded as loud. Durand swung his Colt out. Before his gun, in the doorway, stepped a broad figure.

"Hold that gun, Durand," said a razor-sharp voice.

So Matt Braden had finally come.

Chapter Ten

Braden advanced within the lamplight, his broad, powerful hands hanging loosely, his dark-visaged face set and sullen. Durand seemed frozen, Colt still slanting across at Braden.

Braden said softly: "Don't be a fool with that gun, Durand, I came up here to talk to you."

In a cold voice that whipped across the room like a flashing knife, Durand said: "Come to tell me who murdered Larry Cramer?"

Ignoring the thrust, Braden rested his big hands near his guns and in his heavy, belligerent way replied: "I'm here to make you a proposition . . . I want you to throw in with me."

"You've got more nerve than sense. I don't consider that a compliment."

"Look at it any way you like. It's a pure business deal. You're too damned swift with a gun to be on the other side. There's not a man this side of Red River who can match you, unless it's Kane or me. I can use your services. I need your guns, your savvy of men and horses."

"You know my answer."

"No, I'm waiting."

The big man's black eyes bored into Durand like gimlets and a thin-lipped smile cut crookedly across his dark, broad face, revealing white, flashing teeth. And Durand, feeling the power of this man beat against him in a great flood, understood now how he held a tough, hard-bitten crew of border fighters together, how he whipped them into a smooth organization. Braden radiated power unlike any man Durand had ever encountered. Was it fear? His first fear of a man?

"You're a damned fool if you turn me down," Braden said

103

at last, letting his words sink in.

"Then I'm a damned fool. You knew I'd refuse before you asked me."

Mockingly Braden said: "You're a bigger fool than I thought possible. For a man swift with his guns, you're slow in the head. You'll never leave this country alive." As he spoke, Braden stepped backward to the door, and wheeled and rushed from the room, leaving behind him the wake of his violent threats.

Durand could not shoot a man in the back, so he stared after Braden for a moment. Then, in sudden realization, came a fearful feeling—the horses! Braden's presence in town meant only one thing—he had come after the horses. And it was suddenly clear to him that Braden, knowing his offer would be refused, had deliberately come to the hotel to hold Durand while Kane and his men made their bid for the remuda bunched at the corral.

Durand blew out the lamp, waited for his eyes to accustom themselves to the change, and stepped into the darkened hallway. At the far end, light from the lobby broke the darkness. For an instant, like a swift shadow, a man stood against the light. Was it Braden? Abruptly a gun flashed and its quaking *boom* beat against the hall's thin boarding, filling the passageway with its thunder. Durand fired, too, but he knew he had missed, like the gunman who had triggered as he lunged cat-like for the stairs. Durand ran down the long hall. At the top of the stairs, his hard gaze swept the lobby, found it empty. And, taking the steps in long strides, he raced out to the verandah.

No one there. Braden had vanished.

As Durand started down the street, the ominous rattle of gunfire broke out in an angry growl from the east where the corrals lay. That quickened him to full stride now, past men appearing cautiously from saloons. The guns' full-throated roar grew heavier—short, vicious blasts that carried a familiar, foreboding note. Past blacked-out buildings he ran, and, when Luke Givins's big barn loomed in front, he cut to his left, sprinting on a straight line for the corral some fifty yards away. But a new fear flayed him, for the guns no longer growled, and a troubled silence reigned over the corrals and sheds. Where were Wyatt's men? Durand slowed, then froze. The corral was empty; so recently had it been emptied that the pungent smell of dust churned up by nervous horses clung heavily in the night air. The corral's gate hung loosely open, and near it he stumbled over a soft object. It was one of Wyatt's riders, sprawled face down in the thick dust, gun in one hand. Durand cursed and began a circle of the corral, dreading further discoveries. As he swung to the far side, a man suddenly rose from the ground, weaving on his feet. Durand rushed up—found Jim Wyatt stumbling like a drunken man, head bent in pain, staggering. At that moment, men came rushing from the street, the *clanking* of spurs ringing clearly above their excited voices, and, lashing through their talk like a bull-whip, came Luke Givins's bitter cursing. While the crowd milled curiously, someone found another Wyatt man crumpled alongside a shed.

After the first outburst of talk over the corral battle, the men from the street fell silent and soon began drifting back to the saloons. Doc Gates, Red Cloud's hard-drinking gunshot wound specialist, arrived in a hurry when called from his customary place at the Osage Girl bar. Durand noticed scant sympathy in this crowd; its members read the portent of tonight's fight without any need of interpretation. Matt Braden had come shooting for the horses as they knew he would, and he had won them back. A man might challenge him, but succeeding in it was another thing. Matt Braden was still king of

105

the town so far as they were concerned.

Later, in Givins's tiny office, as Wyatt nursed a bullet-gashed head, a council of war got under way. The lamplight made a fearsome figure of the Texan, with his long yellow hair showing incongruously above Doc Gates's generous bandages, his blue eyes cold and flashing and unwavering, a fighting man who was shaken but not beaten.

"Tell us what happened, Jim," Durand said. "I'm more responsible for this than anyone. When I went to the hotel, Braden made me a proposition. He knew I wouldn't take him up, so I figure it was made to slow me down, keep me there, while the main bunch jumped you and the boys at the corral. I say that because they tried to get me when I started to come back down here."

Wyatt shook his head, trying to control his voice. "They sent about fifteen men down on us at the corral," he began angrily. "I'll swear we got two, but they had us spotted an' the boys never had a chance against that many guns. Just too many guns, that's all." He touched his head in weariness and bitter memory. "Last thing I remember . . . they rushed the gate and something hit me."

He strode across the room and swung back, half stumbling, his anger blazing at white heat. "I lost a good man," he said soberly, "got another crippled. But, by God, they'll pay for every bullet. I'll track down every Braden rider who had a hand in this!"

"Hold on," Durand broke in. "You're not fit to rush out of here tonight or tomorrow. Doc Gates says you can't ride for a couple of days. Now you give me a man or two, and we'll bring those hosses back and Braden's scalp."

"I'm goin' with you."

Givins spat carefully through the open doorway and went over to Wyatt with the studied calmness of an older man.

"Durand's right, Jim," he said. "Don't pull out of here like a reckless fool. Mebbe that's just what they want you to do. So you'd leave yourself open for an easy drygulching. Send a man with Durand as he says. You won't be any good on a rough trail for a couple of days."

Wyatt stood with head bent, hard eyes wandering, his mouth set in a stubborn line. At last, he relaxed and said reluctantly: "All right, mebbe I'm not thinkin' straight tonight. But let's don't dally around."

"We'll leave tonight," Durand said.

"Charlie Worth will be your man. Good shot an' tracker, cool in a gun battle. He rode out to a Texas camp south of town to see about more hands. My outfit's pretty well shot up now. We need more men. Charlie ought to be back *pronto*."

Durand saddled, packed his horse, and waited at the stable. After an hour, with Worth still not in appearance, he drifted outside. Givins had taken Wyatt to his home for the night. Angry gusts of wind swooped down the street, befitting his mood. Again the town lay shrouded in silence, its evil hidden by the night, he thought. But there would be lively talk in the saloons about Braden's coup, accomplished in convincing six-gun style, with one man killed, two wounded. Power like that, ruthlessly displayed, meant something in a town like Red Cloud. Another man had risen to buck the king and had fallen short in a showdown. Yet tonight's episode had further crystallized Durand's feelings. He wanted to meet Braden and Kane, man to man, in a test where swiftness of hand and wrist and eye would decide the issue. And, like a flashing signal, ran a foreboding train of thoughts mixed with an unaccountable urging to see Ellen Winston. Tonight all the dark facets of Red Cloud and Braden and Kane rippled through him in continuous warning. This line of heavy reasoning was new to him, and he had never known it until he had met the girl. She offered the only light, the only hope, save for his guns and those death messengers were lacking, holding only a hollow victory that had to be repeated over and over. This time, he felt with the keen awareness of a man wise to the border and the Territory, men would die under flaming guns when he and Charlie Worth rode north.

This dark thinking jarred him. Was she the cause? He shifted nervously, trying to drive out this weakness. His heavy spurs tinkled musically as he moved, and, when he looked up the street, a figure came toward him. His pulse quickened. It was a woman—Ellen Winston. In the gloom, she looked soft and appealing, and the old weakness ran through him like a rising torrent. Neither spoke for a long moment.

"I heard about the shooting," she said haltingly. "I wondered if you were in it."

He laughed a laugh streaked with irony. "I'd be feeling better if I had been in it. They rode down on the corral while I was at the hotel. Killed one of Wyatt's riders, shot up another, and winged Jim."

He heard her quick gasp. She said: "There was shooting at the hotel. Dad heard the shots from his room. But the place was empty when he ran out."

"That's right. Somebody shot at me. I shot back. We both missed. Guess it was Braden. He paid me a short call before the shooting."

"Matt came up to see you?"

"None other. That was before the shooting at the corrals. By the time I ran down here, the horses were gone. It was a pretty thorough job. If Braden hadn't delayed me, we might have avoided this."

"That means," she pondered, "that Matt's men got the horses?"

"Who else would try it?" Durand said sharply, stung by

the fact that she would even question it. "Maybe he wasn't in the gang that shot up Wyatt's boys, but they were his riders . . . men in his pay. That makes him as guilty as the men who did the killin'. He's no better than the lowest bush-whacker who rides and shoots for him."

"You speak with a terrible conviction."

"I say that because I know it's true. I feel that as keenly as I do your presence here tonight."

Was she trying to protect Braden? Why did she always seem to doubt evident facts about the man? Suspicion seeped through him then, as it had the night on the prairie, and he hardened into a steel-like stand, shutting her off from him, making himself oblivious of her eyes, her mouth, her hair, her sweetness and softness. A short time before, he would not have thought that possible. He had hungered for her, for the sound of her voice, for the feel of her hands. She represented all that he had missed, all that he had longed for over the hard, bitter years. She was a vision that he had gazed at hazily across smoky campfires when he rode alone, a dim picture and hope that had become an amazing reality. Now that vision was dissolving like a mirage. Perhaps at the start he had no right to hope for her; perhaps she vas something to be viewed only from a distance. He turned away, staring off, un-seeing.

Then, from afar, it seemed, he heard her murmur: "I'm not trying to stop you from doing what you believe is right, what you feel you must do. But I don't want you to lose your-self in this . . . this endless fighting. It'll go on and on . . . until more men are killed . . . until perhaps you. . . ."

He turned and faced her, feeling the pull of her soft, ear-nest voice, again aware of her closeness, feeling the shock of it, and his suspicion began drifting away. "I can't stop," he said. "My best friend's been killed. I have a pledge to keep for him. I had a job to do here before they got Larry. Now it's more binding than ever. Jim Wyatt has lost in this, too, and I can't let him down. Not a man with his heart. He's lucky to be alive." With cold decision, he went on: "I'd die before I let a man down. I can't quit. If I quit, I couldn't live with myself. And you wouldn't want me and no man would ride with me . . . because I wouldn't be a man."

He towered above her in the gloom, a hardened man, unshakable, bound to a powerful code. In his voice she had read, again, the return of all the overwhelming despair she had seen in him the day Larry Cramer was buried under the sod of Red Cloud's little boothill. It was as if a stranger stood before her, a man in whom there was no softness, no kindly nature; yet she knew this was not the Walt Durand who had grinned at her from behind a dead horse, not the man who had chided her good naturedly about her riding.

She said: "I wouldn't stop you if I could. Then you would hate yourself and me. But why should you go on like other men? To be shot down in a dark alley . . . to be found like Larry Cramer."

"That's the chance I'll have to take," he said. "But I'm willing to take it."

She had moved nearer him, until she stood close and haunting, all of her before him, waiting. And a tremor shook him, and he was struggling in a great whirlpool and Ellen's face shone through the mist. . . .

From down the street, clear and ringing in the still night, came the rapid hammer of a horse traveling at a dead run. Durand, watching now, saw the dark blob of horse and rider pounding toward the stable. He led Ellen farther into the shadows, and she caught his instant alertness, felt the hard grip of his fingers on her arm pulling her behind him. The rider checked the horse in a cloud of swirling dust, dismounted, took two jangling steps toward the stable's office, and then turned suspiciously at sight of the two figures.

"Who's that?" he asked warily, stepping back as a gun blurred magically in his right hand.

Durand stepped out unhurriedly. "Ease up, Charlie . . . it's Durand."

Charlie Worth's slow, drawling voice dropped its edge, revealed its ready relief. "Good. Didn't know you in the dark. You've got to play it safe in this man's town. How well I know. I'm looking for Jim. Seen him? What's up?"

Briefly Durand told him and about the agreement to go after the horses. Worth's muttering curse leaped out at the news. "By gawd, Durand, we've got our work cut out for us. I was afraid of that. That's why I went for help. When do we ride?"

"Tonight. Soon as you're ready."

"All I need is a fresh hoss. Damn the luck! I couldn't round up any extra men. Tried a camp 'way south of here, but they was all out with the herd except the cook. I left word an' maybe some'll come in tomorrow to reinforce Jim. They're Texans, like us. If I hadn't been away . . . ," he complained bitterly, self-accusingly.

Durand looked at Ellen, but she didn't hear. Then he led his horse from the stable out in front, feeling the tightness inside him mounting. He recinched the saddle and the horse grunted and shifted his feet. Durand wanted to linger here as long as possible, it seemed. It was a dense, weakening feeling and he fought against it. Shortly now Charlie Worth appeared leading one of Givins's horses. Both animals were packed lightly, with carbines strung across each saddle.

Breathing deeply, Durand swung into the saddle. But he did not ride off immediately. Instead, he was held here for a moment by Ellen looking up at him silently, intently, resignedly. Sparse light breaking from the stable office threw her face into soft, appealing outline, framing her as he would never forget, combining with the shadows to forge a further mystery about her. Tonight he had been on the brink of discovering her, and, as always, something had intervened, checkmating him. And, he thought fleetingly, until he followed this grim trail to its bloody finish he would never discover her, never know her.

She said—"Good luck."—and her voice sounded low and distant.

"I'll be back."

Charlie Worth flung his lean body into the saddle and they trotted off around the stable toward the corrals. Durand did not look back, but seared in his memory rose a haunting face touched softly by light. He wondered if he would see her again.

Watching them whirl away, Ellen Winston was struck again by Durand's actions as they had met and talked here tonight—by his hardness, by the set lines in his face, by the stony glittering in his gray eyes. She half ran past the building to follow them as long as she could see. Hoof beats deadened as they made vague, rapidly moving blobs for a short time, then melted into the darkness—two grim hunters, traveling the dark trail.

When she finally went aimlessly up the vacant street, swept by a dull, mournful wind whistling sullenly around the squat frame buildings, she felt a heavy sensation of weariness and isolation, mingled with dread and fear for Walt Durand.

Chapter Eleven

It was close to daybreak, with an early grayness routing the night, before Durand and Worth paused to water their horses and cook breakfast at a shallow, tree-rimmed creek that skirted the first huge roll of hills. Here at the creek the herd of horses had also been watered. Braden's riders had boldly followed the main trail north from Red Cloud, and, sketched by the light night, the broad clutter of hoofs could be followed.

As he dismounted, Worth scowled and commented: "Guess they figured they wouldn't be chased. Just stuck to the main trail."

"They'll cut off north of here somewhere in rough country," Durand predicted. "That's when we'll have to look sharp for an ambush. They may drop riders behind to hole up along the trail and watch."

In silence they headed north, still on the main trail, which looped higher through wooded upland. At several points they found where groups of horses had made dashes from the main bunch, but apparently the wilder ones had been turned back by the close-riding horsemen. At each twist of the trail, Durand and Worth slowed down, scouting the brush carefully, eyeing the high places and bends.

Before midday they found where the riders had turned the remuda off the trail to the east where the rocky hills stacked up roughly and the timber grew denser. This sector, too broken for grazing big herds, offered ambush for the unwary horseman. An hour's ride from the turning-off place, the two halted. Looking down the rugged trail, Durand said: "We're getting close, Charlie. These tracks don't look more'n a few hours old."

They dismounted to look closer at the tracks. "I can almost smell dust." Worth laughed. "Or maybe it's trouble I smell."

Before moving on, they checked their guns and unloosened their saddles to let the horses blow for a while. Off in the timber, the sharp call of birds rang out; about a quarter mile eastward buzzards circled and dived in an overcast sky. Both men looked at the wheeling vultures and the same thought struck them. "You know it's odd," Charlie Worth said slowly, "that we haven't found nothin' but hoss tracks. Remember you said Jim recalled hittin' two men at the corral."

They went on, slower now, the *creak* of saddle leather and the dull rap of hoofs the only sound in this heavy hill country. They trotted up an incline thick with brush and down a rock-strewn descent where the trail angled across a dry wash. Not far away the circling buzzards, sighting the men and horses, wheeled away. Suddenly Durand's horse shied violently against Worth's mount. Off to the left side of the trail a man lay in the close-growing brush, his hat over his face. Afoot, they looked at him and removed the travel-stained hat, apparently the last bare ministration of the riders who had left him here.

"He rode as far as he could," Worth said. "Then they dumped him, took his hoss. Fine outfit. Don't even bury their dead. I reckon this shows Jim Wyatt still shoots straight. I'm surprised he got this far."

They replaced the hat and rode on, down and up, following the rough slashes through the hills. Gradually the timber lessened and Durand sighted familiar country. When he turned to Worth, a troubled frown on his face, he said: "Should be up with them now. Were traveling faster. Look sharp."

Overhead the sky was switching abruptly from its overcast

to a darker hue and clouds commenced rolling darkly and wind began whipping out of the north, carrying a faint bite of dampness and cold.

"Charlie," said Durand, "it's about time they watered that bunch. There's a deep creek past that biggest hump of hills yonder. If we don't catch up there, we may have to go clear to Braden's headquarters."

They rode at a gallop then without let-up until the line of hills came upon them. Climbing to a slender cut, Durand felt the dampness increase as the wind got stouter and lashed the timber; in the distance thunder made its threatening clap and the sky darkened. They stopped to look and Worth muttered aloud as, directly beyond where a creek cut across a shallow valley, horses moved like phantoms in the rapidly gathering storm. At the rim of the half circle on this side of the creek, several horsemen bulked, guarding against any breaks for liberty by the half-wild animals.

"There they are," said Durand quietly. "This storm is making them hard to handle. If Braden's men are smart, they'll hold them there until this blows over. Let's hope they do. When the storm heads, we can move in."

"I'd call this a right fortunate break in the weather for us," Charlie Worth said dryly.

As they waited, making their plans, a light rain whipped by a rushing wind began pattering down; soon it formed a slanting, silvery sheen. Peering through the screen, they glimpsed riders bunching the horses into the trees framing the creek. They were going to hold them there.

When the wind seemed to reach its height and the rain fell in great furious sheets, the two men moved from the cut and down into the storm-swept valley. They were wet to the hide now, but the radical turn in the weather was providing them with an unlooked for opportunity: to bid for the horses before the riders shoved deeper into rougher country. The enveloping screen of rain would mask their movements until they moved in close to the heavily guarded remuda.

For several hundred yards, they were lost in the semi-blackness and downpour, but soon vague shapes loomed out. First a moving horseman, then trees, then more horses. Dimly a rider whirled his horse to cut back a skittish mustang, and to the left Durand noticed more riders closely spaced on the near side of the creek. He and Worth reined to their right now and the horsemen faded from sight. When the trees, groaning under the whiplash of the storm, came into view, they were at the southernmost edge of the horse herd. So they moved north, intending to drive the horses through the ring of riders back onto the hill trail. Shaggy-maned, lean-limbed horses began plunging wildly under the groaning trees, moving in nervous rushes. And as the motion was transmitted swiftly to others and the whole herd suddenly commenced moving, shouts cut through the wind, joining the dull pounding of charging hoofs.

Durand pressed forward eagerly, shouting now, Worth beside him, and the dark masses swirling before them, gathering speed in the glowering darkness. Suddenly, tearing up from one side at a run, came a rider bent on turning the animals back. He swept past, shouting something to Durand and disappeared in the swelling darkness. The remuda was running now, full force for the break in the hills. Through the dimness, black as ebony, Durand caught a second's glimpse of a massive leader striking straight ahead. It was the black stallion, and Durand thrilled as he saw the muscled marvel lunging out like the spearhead of a cavalry charge. Like a black bolt the stallion was running; he disappeared in the gloom and the others followed sweepingly after him. Riders' coarse shouts fell off as they strung out to head off the swift-striding avalanche. Deep-rooted elation swept over Durand as he thought again of the magnificent black, his heaving muscles, the wild sweep of his shaggy mane, like a black mantle. The stallion had led his followers toward the hills like a field marshal leading a dash across a bullet-spattered field. And not a Braden man was mounted to match the black and head him off. *With luck,* Durand thought fast, *we can follow them through . . . if the storm holds and. . . .*

Veering through the storm came the warning hammer of approaching riders. In the glistening dimness, like grim specters, rode two men.

A pistol barked flat and dull. Durand and Worth jabbed spurs to flanks and cut off at an angle to lose the pair. It became evident quickly that this would be a race. The riders kept boring in, pulling closer. Water glistened on horseflesh as Durand looked back. Beside him, Worth exploded with a Rebel-like whoop, waving a big black gun. They opened up on the lead rider, and, as they did, explosions flattened out behind them. Suddenly the nearest man flung up his arms and rolled limply from the saddle. The second man's horse staggered woodenly, fell from sight, and Durand and Worth rode after the stallion's streaking subjects.

The rush from the creek timber, the black's contagious sprint, and the short-lived riders' attack had flashed before Durand in a few seconds, although the fiery scroll of action, with its veiled, sinister movements in this rain-curtained scene, might have unfolded timelessly, so vague did men and horses loom as in a slow-moving dream.

They rode straight for the slash in the hills that yawned down into the little valley. Here would be the stiffest test— facing riders left behind by the stallion's lightning run. As they neared the rocky trail leading up the incline, little knots of horsemen blurred out through the silver-streaked mantle.

For long moments there was only the muffled *clatter* of hoofs against rocks as they labored uphill on the rough footing. Beyond, dimly, like plunging, long-maned wraiths, the last of the stallion's bunch raced violently up to the mouth of the defile. At the same time, shapes of horsemen straggling along both sides of the trail cropped out more distinctly.

As Durand and Worth, bent low in their saddles, swept after the horses, a warning shout rose from behind them and guns made their *boom* above the storm's dull roar. Near the hill's crest, where the cut was narrowest, the horses were forced to slow their dash between the crowded walls. Durand and Worth, behind them, pressed toward the plunging, rearing, wavering mass, shouting and urging them on, and, like a black flood suddenly released, the horses spurted forward and the top was gained.

Durand and Worth turned at the crest and looked back down into the gloom-filled cut, waiting. And in a few seconds it came—the pounding of riders up the steep, rock-pitted grade. The gun in Durand's right hand flickered flame as the first horseman bobbed menacingly through the thickness. Horse reared and rider fell. Behind them came others, and now Charlie Worth's gun joined in warmly to smash them back. Another rider toppled drunkenly; a wounded horse, screaming, threw threshing front hoofs high, tilted backward, and crashed against an oncoming rider. No more riders appeared and the crest's defenders raced back on the trail. Somewhere ahead the herd thundered with the black stallion as its wild spearhead.

Durand's high elation suddenly dimmed as he glanced at Charlie Worth. The man's right arm was drawn up and his sleeve dripped red. Durand pulled up and, pointing to the arm, shouted encouragement. Worth's bearded face broke into a set, forced grin. Around a sharp bend they reined up.

There were no signs of close pursuit for the moment.

"Charlie," Durand said tensely. "Tail the hosses on to the main trail and push south. I'll follow . . . hold them off until you get free of the hills. If they get past me, let the remuda go and shift for yourself. Can you hold on?"

The Texan nodded. "Hell, yes! Just tie somethin' around this arm. But what about you?" he asked as Durand bound the arm with his bandanna.

"I can take care of myself. Now you ride like hell and watch sharp. This weather'll cover you a while."

Worth hesitated, not liking this lone rear guard business. "I ain't leavin' you to do my fightin'," he insisted stubbornly.

"You're not. You've got a man-size job ahead of you. Better hurry . . . and whatever you hear, go on. I'll catch you. Just keep those horses moving."

"Damned if you ain't a stubborn cuss, but this is no time for a debate. All right. See you in Red Cloud."

Worth plunged down the trail and faded out abruptly, lost in the swirling tempest. Durand reloaded and sat his horse for several minutes, listening and watching. Although the storm still raged, he sensed a gradual change. The rain was slowly lessening. With no sound from beyond the bend, he turned westward on Worth's fleeting tracks. At intervals he paused to listen and look back. Silence still covered the timbered trail and he rode on again, with the hope stirring him that the piece of sharp shooting at the cut had stopped further pursuit. He rode over a humped-up hill through scraggly timber and down into a box-like cañon slabbed roughly with rock. Here he pulled up in timber off the trail.

Minutes raced past without foreign sounds stirring above and back on the trail. The rain had dropped off to a slow patter, and, partly sheltered here, the force of the wind was blunted. *Charlie Worth is right,* he told himself. *I'm stubborn as*

119

hell. For within him, growing stronger, was the wish to meet Braden or Kane or the others. He saw with a swift clarity now that only guns could settle this, and the feeling of doubt and indecision, tinged with a faint, new fear that had touched him strangely at Red Cloud, was routed. With ease he could ride out of the cañon and catch Worth and the horses. But something held him here. He knew horsemen would be coming presently, that this was better than being ham-strung from behind out in the open, that this was the surest way to give Charlie Worth, with one good arm, a fighting chance. And he thought: *She is right, too. A trouble hunter, sure. But this country would be better for the men who hunted down trouble, faced it, and smashed it. And there was Larry Cramer . . . that night in Abilene. . . .*

So he waited there in the scrawny, dripping timber, his gaze slanting upward at the rocky path that dropped down into the cañon less than 100 yards away. During the swift ride he had not seen Braden and somehow he doubted that the range boss rode with these riders. Although Braden would plan the coups, ordinarily he did not take a hand in their execution, Luke Givins had told him. But Kane and Crawford and Edmund?

Presently he became aware of a distant *clatter:* hard hoofs on rocky footing. The sounds fell off, then returned, came closer. Durand pulled his horse where he could sweep the entire trail with his eyes. Now the sounds picked up, drumming nearer. And in a rush, dark, glistening figures of men and horses filled the top of the trail where it sloped down sharply. Durand, motionless, a lean man in sodden clothes, waited.

Now the horsemen—he counted four—rushed down the trail. In the lead, as they gained the cañon's floor, rode Smoke Crawford, black eyes sweeping the jumble of rocks and timber with the all-seeing gaze of a vulture. They came forward briskly; Durand moved into the center of the trail.

Crawford's head lifted in quickening surprise, eyes glittering and wide in amazement. He yanked his horse back. "Durand!" he said sharply, with a killer's eagerness. "God damn you!"

And as if in a long-rehearsed drama, Durand caught the stiffening of Crawford's wiry body, the familiar downward, darting blur of hand for gun. Explosions filled the cañon. Durand heard his Colt bellow first, saw Crawford falling from the saddle, his smoking gun pointed downward. Durand pulled twice at the other riders. One pitched forward onto the neck of his frightened horse; another, gun spurting flame, clutched his chest and fell from the saddle with a stunned and clouded gaze. Horses were rearing and plunging in the mêlée. Beside the trail, the fourth rider fired coolly and deliberately as he sought to handle a jerking horse, and one of these shots tore into Durand like a hot iron. In a gathering haze before his eyes, he saw the rider pivot the horse and wheel back and up, out of the narrow cañon. Vaguely he wondered why he had not shot at the fleeing man, then he realized he could not lift his gun. The haze had become a fog. . . .

Walt Durand's face, set and grim and cold under wide-brimmed hat, dug into Charlie Worth's thoughts as he drummed along the trail that lay smothered in a swirling, gray blackness. He remembered snatches of what Jim Wyatt had said about Durand—his warmness, his steady coolness, his record as a manhunter, his speed and timing with a gun. Above all, he had been struck by an indefinable grim sadness about the man. He thought: *Maybe manhunters get that way, yet Durand is no killer.*

His horse was laboring after the long run and he stopped.

Behind him no new sounds cut across the storm's enveloping roar and he spurred ahead after a short pause. The trail slanted downward and a box-like cañon yawned before him. Clambering up its far side, he looked back again, saw and heard nothing but the storm, and rode on. A growing numbness in his arm bothered him now, but it grew not worse and he could handle the horse with his left. As yet he had encountered none of the stragglers, and he began to wonder if the bunch had cut off the main trail. But, as he turned the course over carefully in his mind, he could not recall a branching trail. He became aware then that he way still thinking of Durand back there and not the horses; he had not even inspected the trail thoroughly as he should have, so he bent over in the saddle to examine it. Immediately he saw the marks of many hoofs. And 'about half a mile from the cañon, as he rounded a bend, he caught up with the tail-enders. Bunching them, he urged them on until the main body of the remuda took shape. There was a let-up, a falling off, in the storm now, a faint clearing, and he found the main bunch moving slowly behind the stallion. When the stragglers closed up, the leader threw up his head, quickened his stride, and the remuda was once more on the move.

Charlie Worth was congratulating himself on his luck when out of the east, behind him, broke the low, chatter of guns. *Durand!* He pulled up, a deadening fear running through him, the significance of what he had heard weightily and fully upon him. The shots came close together, dull and threatening, wafting their warning. It sounded like close-range work to his practiced ears. He sucked in his breath as the firing fell off, then died completely. And he remembered again, with a helpless, sickening feeling, the tall, gray-eyed man sitting a beaten horse on a rocky trail, waiting.

Chapter Twelve

Durand's urging to go on ran in Charlie Worth's mind.

He looked from the retreating horses back toward the cañon, hesitating. With a lunge he suddenly spurred back down the trail. He had changed his mind. *To hell with the horses!* He could pick them up later. When, at last, the trail bent downward where it cut into the cañon's wall, he stopped and gazed down. Near the center a riderless horse moved. He plunged downtrail, the old fear returning, for his quick eyes had seen a man's body sprawled among the rocks. Here on the rock-studded flooring ruled a silence that fanned his dread at what he might discover. He peered down at the man, quick relief flooding over him. It was not Durand. Another rider lay loosely, like an emptied sack, farther down the trail. A few paces away, Worth saw a third man, prone, stir feebly. Dismounting, he went over to him and looked at an unfamiliar face, ashen and glazed and bewildered with its life slipping swiftly away. The man's lips moved and Worth bent over to catch the words.

"Never saw such shootin' . . . gawd he was fast . . . Crawford looked ordinary."

Worth eased the dying man's head, aware that it was but a matter of minutes now, perhaps seconds.

"Shore, I'm through," came the far-away admission. "Rough trail . . . mighty rough."

When the lips stopped moving, Worth stood up. Three dead men cluttered the cañon, and one of them, as he lay dying, had muttered in amazement and bewilderment at the speed of Durand's gun. Relief and hope came back. But where was Durand? Worth mounted and covered the entire

123

cañon's bottom to make certain. After giving the place one last careful inspection, he raced up the outgoing trail after the horses. . . .

Red Kane was raking in his second straight pot at a back table when Matt Braden entered the Osage Girl and crossed over to him, his heavy silver spurs jangling. Braden nodded at Kane and went on to a back room. Kane followed him back shortly.

Braden said: "Sit down, Red. Let's talk."

Kane eased his bulky body into a chair and muttered: "Anything wrong? We got the hosses all right, didn't we?" He was smiling and cocky, in rare good humor.

Braden nodded through rolling smoke. "You got the horses all right, but I hear Durand hit the trail after 'em, night before last."

Kane's good humor vanished. "What if he did?" he demanded. "What can one man do?"

"He wasn't lone-wolfing it this time. Another man went with him. One of those Texas boys."

"We handled the Texans at the corral," Kane ventured with a thin smile. "What can two men do against that big bunch of riders with the hosses? Not a damn' thing, Matt," he said, answering his own question. "Them boys can shoot."

Braden seemed to be studying a knot in the rough lumber wall over Kane's head. "So can Durand."

Kane's anger blazed up. He demanded sullenly: "What's eatin' you, Matt? We got the hosses. What else do you want? The moon?"

"Don't roar like a bull," Braden warned. In a low tone, he said: "I tried to bluff Durand out the other night and it didn't take. Now we've got to finish him."

"You said that before," the foreman said dryly. "Why

didn't you tackle him that night?"

"I did. We both missed in the dark."

"Well, am I supposed to take him bare-fisted, out in the open, in the brush, or where?"

"Pick a spot to your liking. But lay off the close-in fist fighting . . . he's too tough for you."

Braden knew the remark would inflame Kane and he watched the foreman's face crimson with anger, saw his cold eyes glitter. "I'd beat him easy without his tricks," Kane stormed, "an' he's never faced a gun fast as Red Kane's."

The man's ego was his weak point, Braden had learned long ago, and now he played on that. "I been hearing more about Durand lately," Braden said. "Seems some of the boys remember him at Abilene and Hunnewell. He cleaned out some tough ones. They say he's quick as a cat with that gun, though that don't mean he can match you. That's something a man never knows till he tries. That's what urges a gun slinger on and on . . . till he bumps up against some fellow whose lightning has more forks in it."

Kane's anger had eased off to studied, suspicious appraisal of his boss. "You're mighty anxious for me to meet Durand. Fair enough. But it's my neck, not yours, up for stake."

Braden said: "If you can't handle it, I'll get somebody that can."

Kane stood up. "I'll meet him, but I'll pick the time and the place. You can be damned sure it'll favor Red Kane. I'm not afraid of any man that ever slung a hog-leg, includin' you!"

As the foreman stamped from the room, Braden knew that he had figured Kane right. True, the man feared nothing; his insurmountable ego, stemming from successful though hard-bitten years in border towns, and his tremendously powerful

125

body, gave him an iron-bound confidence in his ability to drive men, to whip them down. Braden was smiling when he left the room, and he *clanked* to the long bar and ordered whiskey for the house, so good did he feel. After that, he pushed the swinging doors aside, stepped out into the sun-bright street, and watched riders jog past. He had been conscious of new respect—or was it fear?—among the townspeople and saloon regulars since he had won back the horses, and that awareness revived the old sense or sureness that had always characterized him.

About noon Braden walked up to the hotel and ate dinner. Before he left the dining room, Ellen Winston had agreed to ride with him that afternoon. He had caught the hesitancy in her eyes, but she had accepted and that was enough for him. For the first time in his life, he knew that he was in love with a woman. She had affected him strangely. Of late he had noticed a growing urge to break away from the gang, although he had discounted that as a weakness engendered by a woman's softness. He waited impatiently until time for the ride, and, when they left Red Cloud behind with its dust and damp-smelling deadfalls, he was glad to be away from the sweat of men and their loud, boisterous talk. They talked sparingly, letting the horses decide their pace, and the sun beat down with its flooding heat. About an hour later they dismounted at a spring shaded by tall cottonwoods. Braden watched her intently, noting her subdued expression, her quietness—this was new to him and, in quick calculation, he thought of Durand.

"Ellen," he began, picking his words with care, "I didn't finish what I had to say to you the other night at the hotel." He laughed lightly, explaining: "My foreman interrupted me."

No smile or change of expression answered him and he felt

puzzled again. Ordinarily her laughter was ringing and quick.

"I believe you said what you thought pretty well," said Ellen calmly.

"No," he added gently. "I didn't finish."

She made no answer, nothing to draw him on, and in his confident way he had not expected this. He stood near her, speaking earnestly: "Ellen, I want you to marry me. Is that strong enough? Does that show how I feel about you?"

She looked away, past him, her features tightening. There was no instant brightness there, no eagerness as he had hoped, half expected. Her lack of response stung him; it was like a whiplash to his proud nature. "I want you to marry me," he repeated. "I love you. . . . That's all any man can say, isn't it? What else can I say to you?" For the first time, he thought he saw a softness in her eyes, and he said quickly: "Give me your answer, Ellen." And he caught hold of her in his eagerness and held her. He kissed her once, twice. She did not pull back as before, yet there was no warmth in her and he was the one who stepped back. Her lips were cold and dead to him. He had received his answer without her speaking it, and it rankled him, stung his pride, spurred his hair-trigger anger.

She said: "I can't marry you, Matt. I wouldn't make you a good wife because I don't love you."

"You're sure?"

"Yes."

"What's been going on lately in Red Cloud . . . these shootings . . . would that have anything to do with the way you feel?"

"It might," she said evasively. "But if I loved you, nothing could change me."

"I haven't killed a man," he said.

"I believe you. But who's responsible for the killings? Who plans them? What's happened hasn't been the ordinary run of saloon brawls . . . they're more than that."

She had spoken with ringing conviction, with a hint of suspicion, and he faced her squarely now.

"Who makes up stories to tell you?" Braden demanded. "My hands are clean, I tell you. I'm merely protecting what's mine. Any rancher would do that. If he didn't, he wouldn't last long. You've lived on the border long enough to know that. Now who tells you these stories . . . Durand?"

Her face, at first white and startled, reddened swiftly and he knew that he had guessed correctly. He went on cruelly, all his dammed up hatred of Durand guiding his emotions. "Sure, it's Durand," he said triumphantly. "He's lied about me and my men to save his own killer's hide to look better in your eyes. His soft talk has got you . . . you're like any woman who hears soft words."

Matt Braden's swift metamorphosis from lover to an angry, frustrated man jarred her as he stood before her with blazing hatred of Durand written across his dark, heavy features. He stood outlined in striking vividness, a powerful man whose wrath consumed him like a fire, tempering him to a deadly ruthlessness. She saw a new Matt Braden, and she stepped back. He seemed to be peering through her, and, momentarily, she thought he would reach out for her again. Instead, he eyed her strangely, in a manner that also was new to her, and a disturbing fear of him shook her.

Now he was saying dryly, accusingly: "Guess I know where I stand . . . and the reason for it." He turned, went rapidly to his horse, and mounted. Before he rode off at a gallop for town, he looked at her again in that strange, penetrating way.

She felt frozen until horse and rider disappeared over the fold of a hill. Slowly she mounted, remembering many things—repeated rumors about Braden and his men, their hidden headquarters in the hills, what Durand had said in great bitterness following the bloody corral fight, her father's cold, unvarying, unfriendly attitude toward Braden. She also began recalling little things about Braden that had escaped her before or which she had stubbornly refused to admit she knew—the calculating manner that never left him, even in his love-making, how he commanded men, how he always seemed to be seeing through and beyond her as he had today. His proposal might have been spoken in the same way he ordered a rider to do a chore. The veil around Matt Braden had been lifted, she thought, and she felt a new freedom.

Cal Winston glanced up at her in surprise from his chair when she returned. "Back early, I'd say. Anything wrong?"

"Nothing," she answered. "I merely found out something I should have known long ago."

"Ah, now what could that mean . . . a man?"

"A man I thought I once wanted. I've discovered now I don't want him . . . and I'm surprised it took me this long to find out."

Winston snapped to his feet like a man much younger than his years. "It's taken you a long time, but I knew you would," he said brightly. Then admiringly: "Just like your mother, you are. Once you make up your mind, you're dead right, an' there's no changing it. I know it took me some time to convince her, fine and gallant as I was," he said, smiling.

But through his bubbling elation, she saw a thin line of worry edging his face. "That's the best news I've heard in a long time," he agreed. "But I'm a little worried about Walt Durand. . . . He didn't come back with Jim Wyatt's rider."

Winston led his daughter outside, out of hearing of the clerk, where he continued. "Somehow I don't trust that man. Hears too well and sees too much. I just tolerate him on account of Matt Braden and now maybe I won't do that."

She saw the damaged pride with which he admitted the situation involving Denton, although there was a new and stronger light in his eyes, and he had lost the look of a beaten man managing a bare living from this scarred frontier hotel.

"I never told you, Ellen," he said, "but Braden owns this place, lock, stock, and barrel. I was afraid it might influence you when he asked you to marry him. I wanted you to make your decision with an open mind. Now I can tell you. Guess this means we'll have to move on again, always to another cow town. But I don't mind, if you don't. Your happiness comes first. For that matter, I'm happier, too. I didn't want you to take Braden . . . he's not good enough for you . . . not your kind. I couldn't tell you. You had to make up your own mind. He's a pretty flashy fellow . . . some women like that."

She interrupted: "You're wandering, Dad. What about Walt?"

"Luke got the whole story from Charlie Worth, Wyatt's man. They had a big gunfight in a box cañon east of the main trail. Somehow they got the hosses back an' started for Red Cloud. Charlie got winged an' Durand sent him ahead with the remuda. Charlie was half a mile or so from the cañon when he heard guns. He went back . . . found three dead men . . . all men from Braden's outfit. No sign of Durand anywhere. Charlie figures he got away, but Durand didn't follow the trail after the hosses. So Charlie can't understand how he missed him because he rode back fast. Charlie came on, bunched the hosses in a cañon east of town."

Winston made no attempt to hide what he really thought and his fear became a lively thing, mirrored in his features.

"You said east of the main trail?" Ellen asked. "There's a

trail that angles in from the northeast, from that wild country, to the main road."

She was studying his words, a fear beating rapidly inside her, as she tried to visualize the country.

"Wyatt's got a couple of men out," Winston said feebly, without hope.

She said: "They don't know the country, I do."

"It's not a job for a woman," he said severely.

Charlie Worth lay in bed at Luke Givins's home. Doc Gates, a wizened little man who drank his whiskey at steady intervals, met Ellen and her father at the door. Squinting through thick glasses, Gates said in his always-husky, rasping voice: "A bullet through the fleshy part of his forearm. He'll be up tomorrow. Keep him in bed today, Missus Givins."

Martha Givins, a plump, gray woman with a soft voice, looked after the doctor as he made his way in the direction of saloon row and commented: "That man! You can smell him before you see him. I'm afraid his patients interfere with his drinking."

Cal Winston laughed and said in Gates's defense: "He knows how to treat gunshot wounds and Red Cloud needs him."

Mrs. Givins mumbled in reluctant agreement, and led them into the bedroom.

Charlie Worth, angular and bearded, gazed at them through sunken eyes and said worriedly: "I'm gettin' too much attention . . . it's Walt Durand that needs help, I fear. Should 'a' been here by now. One man can travel faster than one hand pushin' a bunch of hosses."

"Your boys are tryin' to find him," Winston said. "You did a fine job with the hosses, Charlie."

Worth stirred restlessly. He said disconsolately: "Hope

131

they find him." And to Ellen Winston he said: "Now there's a man, Miss Winston. Hosses or guns, he's right in there. He saved my life, I reckon."

Presently Mrs. Givins passed from the room. Ellen sat watching the wounded rider. "You'd better rest and not talk," she said, getting ready to leave.

"Hold up a minute," he said suddenly, stopping her at the door. "What gets me is how I missed him. Maybe he went down the trail. But he wouldn't do that unless he was hurt and out of his head. Somebody who knows the country might find him. Our boys don't know it."

When Ellen finally left the room, a plan was forming in her mind. At the door, she heard her father tell Mrs. Givins: "Believe it'd be safer if we kept quiet about Charlie bein' here. Braden has men in town."

Matt Braden's anger and frustration had simmered down to a dead, positive calmness by the time he rode up to the Osage Girl where horses lined the tie rack. Although sensing in some vague way beforehand what Ellen Winston's answer might be, he had nevertheless held out strong hope for himself. And above the constant uproar created by his riders, as he viewed the possibilities of life with her, he had even hoped for the quiet existence of a settled rancher. He had money, land, and cattle. Now he fully recognized the impossibility of a settled life, and somehow he did not greatly mind. He was a part of the vengeful, give-and-take Territory, he told himself with a touch of pride, and he could not remake himself into something he was not. But burning in his mind was the tall image of Walt Durand. If Durand had not come to Red Cloud? Red Kane, looking at Braden then, would have caught a swift streak of jealousy in his boss's hard-featured face.

Red Kane was lounging in the meager shade of the saloon's front, and went inside at Braden's motion. In the back room again, Kane awaited a reënactment of their meeting earlier in the day.

"I told you," said Braden deliberately, "to get Durand, didn't I? Well . . . forget that . . . he's my man."

Kane's eyes blinked in surprise. "How come? This morning. . . ."

"That was this morning," Braden snapped. "Times change, Red. So do people. He's my man now."

"You changed your mind fast. Fact is you're talkin' like you used to in the old days, Matt. Before you met that Winston gal." Kane's voice held unbounded admiration. "I kinda like the change myself."

Through a rolling haze of smoke, Braden said evenly: "I should have killed him the time we got the tip a U.S. marshal was coming and we shot his horse. She saved his neck then, but today she signed his death warrant."

The foreman said: "I don't get it, Matt."

Braden gave a short laugh. "She turned me down. Turned down Matt Braden, the richest cowman in the country."

"Where does Durand figure in this?" Kane persisted.

Some of his injured pride returned as Braden explained: "He lied to her about me. So he's my man now."

Boots and spurs sounded outside and a man called out softly: "Braden!"

Kane opened the door and a dusty-booted rider jangled in. "What the hell, Shelton," Braden said. "You in a hurry?"

"I was," the rider said lamely. "We lost the horses again and Durand shot hell outta the outfit."

"Durand!"

"Smoke's dead . . . him and two more."

Braden, fire-eyed, grabbed the rider by his shirt front.

Holding him there powerfully, he demanded: "Where's Durand?"

"Got away."

"Got away again! What kind of men do I have?"

Braden pushed Shelton back, knocked over a chair with a savage thrust of one crashing hand, and turned blazing eyes upon his foreman.

"Red, gather up every man and gun we have in Red Cloud. We're goin' north. I want every trail covered like a blanket. Anything that don't look right, shoot it. We're goin' to ride Durand down!"

Chapter Thirteen

Shortly before daybreak Ellen Winston was walking from the hotel through the half light along the empty street to Luke Givins's barn. She wanted to be out of town by sunup and she arrived at the stable a little breathless. A drowsy stable hand nodded at her. Givins was nowhere about, so she went to a stall, brought out her horse, a full-chested sorrel gelding, and saddled him. She mounted and was swinging away from the stable when she sighted Givins coming along the street. He hastened his stiff walk when he saw her, and she waited for him.

He said inquiringly as he came up: "A bit early, Miss Ellen?"

"Perhaps," she said vaguely.

"Still too early for a ride."

She said nothing. Givins, noticing a tenseness she could not entirely hide, glanced up and down the street with his old caution, stepped up beside her horse, and muttered a low warning: "Braden's men rode north last evenin'. From the way they pounded outta town, I'd say they was huntin' trouble. Means only one thing . . . they want Durand. They want him any way they can get him."

He was echoing her fears and she said: "If they find him. . . ."

"Ellen, that's something I don't like to think about."

Suddenly she pressed spurs to the horse and started off. But his sharp question caused her to rein up. "Where you goin', Ellen?" She turned in the saddle, looking down at him determinedly. *A good-looking young woman,* he thought, *and she knows her own mind.*

"North," she said bluntly, and kicked the horse out at a gallop.

Givins, worry wrinkling his face, stood in the street a while after she turned north. Should he tell Cal Winston about this? At length, he decided to say nothing, and went about his early morning chores.

The short savage battle in the box cañon might have been something out of a wandering, patch-quilt dream, and now persistent flashes of that scene kept returning to Durand: Crawford's hard, hawk-like face and its dull surprise abruptly changing as lead knocked the life from his saddle-toughened body; the old habit and warning that had pulled him off the trail and into the timber after coming west out of the cañon. Then he had thought that Charlie Worth would be far down the trail and he could never catch him. . . .

Blackness crawled over him once and he was falling. When he came to, his horse stood a few feet away, reins dragging. He touched his side with one hand; it came away blood stained. Dully he discovered the bloody shirt and one trouser leg. A great desire for water commanded him now. He peered around, saw dripping trees and rocks dancing in a hazy pattern. *No water,* he thought, *no water.* Water was everything. He tried to get a hold on himself, to think this thing out. He wondered how long he had lain here. The storm had passed on. He propped himself up on his good arm, tried to ease up to his feet. He fell back hard. He lay there, his wind coming hard, his chest heaving, sucking in the air. Upon the third effort he made it, swaying and rocking to his feet. He traveled the great distance to the horse and hung there, one arm grasping the saddle horn. Somehow, after an interminable time, he pulled himself up and grunted into the saddle. It was climbing a mountain; his exhaustion was complete; it swept the strength and fight from his body.

At last, he prodded the horse into movement. He knew he was south of the cross-country trail over which Worth had driven the horses. This, he thought with effort, would place him parallel to the main trail angling north from Red Cloud. If he could reach that. . . .

Immediately, in his weariness, he wanted to doze in the saddle. That stirred a fearful feeling. If he fell again, he could never get back upon the horse, and he could not travel afoot. With desperation, he fumbled with the long rope coiled on the right side of his saddle; he passed out again as the effort of tying himself to the saddle returned a surge of blackness. Much later, the abrupt motion of the horse jolted him back to awareness. They were pacing a narrow trail downhill, but now he had lost all direction. He decided to trust the animal's sense of direction, as he could not rely on his own. The timber's encompassing dampness bored into him coldly, and a numbness ran through him, chilling him to the bone, and there came a hotness that spread in waves throughout his body, and the raging thirst sped back and he felt that he was lost. But he could not allow the horse to stop; his only salvation lay in moving.

With a far-away, distant sensation, he knew when night came. And during that night returned the box-cañon scenes: the rush and pounding of horses, Crawford's snarl, and a woman's soft face. The horse plodded on; every motion jolted him, but the bleeding had stopped. Several times, they wandered off the trail, once when Durand ignored the animal's instinct. Each time, however, they angled back to it. Now the trail danced still more weirdly before his eyes, and finally he did not recognize either night or day.

Ellen Winston left the main trail two miles north of Red

Cloud. She was searching for the track that veered in from the northeast. About ten o'clock she found it, a dim, narrow path flanked by close-growing brush—one well-traveled by range riders, it was seldom used now. By afternoon she was deep in these lonely hills, following a muddy beat, and she had not sighted man or animal. This lack of life cast its weight upon her, increased her fear that her mission might be hopeless. She wondered where Wyatt's two riders were, where Braden's men were stalking. She believed, as had her father and Luke Givins, that something had happened to him, that he should have reached Red Cloud by now.

The western sun dropped its flaming red ball lower, and the shadows began lengthening, escorted by a faint tinge of coolness. A creek, running at bank level, barred her path, and she followed it north until she found a likely-looking ford, pushed her horse into the muddy water, and splashed across to the other side. Cutting back, she picked up her route again and pushed ahead.

Suddenly, out of the north, a horseman appeared, then another and another, strung out at short intervals, moving eastward. That sent her back into the cover of the timber. The horsemen stopped, drawing into a tight huddle, so close to her that she heard their indistinct talk. A man gestured to the east with a sweeping arm, and they continued that way, riding slowly and inspecting the ground. They were looking and searching, she saw that. A fear, hard and jolting, crept into her. She had recognized the huge form of Matt Braden among the men. She decided to ride around them, and kicked the horse from the shelter to the west side of the trail. When she had traveled steadily for about half a mile, she cut back eastward to the trail. This placed the riders behind her to the east. She was clear of them for the time and she pressed on fast until the horse began lagging. Her chief danger now, as she saw it, lay in the horsemen doubling back and picking up her tracks.

She stopped to rest the gelding, pausing at the rim of a little park-like clearing and dismounting. The horse went for the short grass and she let him have his way for the moment. All this time she listened and watched. When the sorrel threw up his head and looked uptrail, Ellen looked, too. She saw nothing. The horse went back to the grass, but only for a short time. He raised his head again. Something was moving ahead in the thick tangle of woods. Her first thought was that Braden, always a hard rider, had cut a wide circle and ridden in ahead of her and was working back downtrail. There came a faint noise from the brush. She mounted with hurry, wheeled back out of the opening, and turned to watch. The noise expanded into the slow, deadened *thud* of a horse traveling on rain-softened ground. She expected to see a Braden man burst forth; instead a rangy, ebony-black horse paced into the clearing. His rider, with one hand locked in the shaggy mane, appeared lashed to the saddle.

She gave a little cry and rode forward with a rush. The horse had stopped wearily near the center of the park, his burden motionless, slumped forward. Now she was down and grabbing the reins and looking up into the slack, ashen face of Walt Durand. She started to loosen the rope and ease him to the ground, but with clearing thought she remembered the riders somewhere behind them. Inspecting the rope hurriedly, she saw that Durand was firmly, if awkwardly, tied, so she mounted, took the black's reins and led out westward, her attention shifting rapidly back and forth to Durand's leaden form and the thickly studded timber and brush through which they must travel. Her woman's concern urged her to take Durand from the saddle, to help him, yet reason and caution told her they must press on to a safe distance.

Downgrade they trotted, across a rocky ravine, and up a gradual slope. Upon gaining higher ground, the timber opened up into scattered patches, offering easier travel and less jostling for the wounded man.

At last, a brush-covered cañon beckoned safety and she thought they had gone far enough. There she quickly untied Durand; his loose weight bent her to her knees, and she noticed again the dead grayness of his face. Sight of the bloody shirt hastened her and she dragged him to one side. She was panting in her rapid work and she took the saddle off his horse and bundled the blanket around Durand. But quickly she remembered, opened his shirt, and saw the ugly clotted wound high up on his right chest.

Close to sundown, Durand stirred and mumbled, and Ellen gave him water from her canteen.

She said: "I found you on the trail, hanging on your horse. I've got to get you to Red Cloud, somehow."

Through his weariness, he showed faint interest, but his exhaustion was complete and overpowering and he slept another hour.

When he moved again, she asked: "Can you eat? I packed food." And she repeated to him: "You've got to go to Red Cloud . . . to Doc Gates."

Her meaning seeped slowly through him. "I'll try to ride."

She fed him then. But the food was without taste and he turned his head away. She took the horses to water in the shallow rock pools below the camp, her mind heavy with her problem. When she came back, Durand had propped his head upon a saddle and for the first time he spoke clearly.

"Oh, Walt. . . ." She bent down, and her voice carried a new meaning to him.

He said: "I'll hate to leave this place . . . it's peaceful."

"You'll be strong enough to ride soon. Your fever is gone."

Her concern was etched in her face, in the gray eyes, and he saw her as an appealing woman, mature, yet girl-like.

He said: "Your eyes are tired. You haven't slept."

"I couldn't. Do you think you can ride by morning?"

"I can ride tonight," he answered with a show of spirit.

"No, we'll wait till morning." Her firmness forced him to smile faintly.

"You're the boss," he said. "Your judgment has been good so far." And a new thought struck him wonderingly. "You came out in these hills to find me?"

She told him then about Charlie Worth's arrival, Wyatt's men out searching, her sighting Braden's riders.

Now realization of their position came upon him full force and he lay back, thinking hard. "Then we'd better ride by night," he concluded. "I know this country. Scouted through it when I was hunting Larry. Braden will have men out tomorrow. If I know them, they'll be watching all the trails. No, we'll try it tonight."

Cal Winston paced up and down on the hotel verandah. When riders trotted past in the street, he jumped nervously, inspecting each man keenly, hoping Ellen would be one of them. At eight o'clock his worry drove him downstreet, past cantankerous saloon row, and along to Luke Givins's stable.

Givins came out of his dingy office with a blackened old pipe clutched between his teeth. He was smoking furiously, and, when he spied Winston's anxious face, he knew immediately what plagued the man.

"I'm worried about Ellen," Winston explained. "She left this morning without saying where she was going. I never worry about her because she's been taught to take care of herself, but this is different. She got her horse here, didn't she?"

"She did," said Givins, blaming himself and facing

Winston with a guilty look. "She rode north, Cal. Wouldn't say where to. I tried to stop her, but she whipped that hoss around and rode off. An' I imagine you know why."

"She's headstrong like her mother."

"No, not necessarily that. It's Durand, Cal. That girl went out after him. Can't you piece it together now? He's shot up, I'll bet a new hat."

They parted, agreeing to form a searching party from the townspeople in the morning. Winston made each saloon and carefully noted that not a single Braden rider was in town. There was nothing for him, but waiting, and he walked back to the hotel to watch and wait and curse himself for the full freedom he had displayed with Ellen. Her strong will had always pleased him, for that was a characteristic of her mother, but it also could lead her into a dangerous situation such as this one. His one condoning thought was that she could ride as well as any man and that he had made it a point to teach her self-reliance as he would a son. With all this thinking came a feeling of being old and helpless and alone, and, when he could stand the porch and shadows no longer, he paced heavily through the lobby to his room at the rear of the hotel, scarcely noting Denton, the thin-faced clerk.

In an old trunk Winston rummaged about, finally finding what he sought—an old revolver that had not been fired for years. He held the ancient weapon in his hands, thinking back over the years. Presently it occurred to him that the gun needed cleaning and oiling, and he went about that task with infinite care. Satisfied at length with its condition, he grasped its shiny coldness, which inspired him with new grimness and determination. And then Cal Winston did a thing that was to-tally strange to him for his late years. From the trunk he also retrieved a worn holster and gun belt; these he strapped around him, hanging the holster low. Although he was heavier than when he wore the belt regularly, and it now cut him like a pack horse's cinch, the heavy gun fit snugly in its old position and he strode to the center of the lamplit room and swung his arm down and forward, each time swinging the gun low. He practiced this until his arm ached and his chest heaved. He was satisfied, however, and, when he went noiselessly out and down the short hallway to plant a suspicious gaze on Denton, he moved with the spring of a younger man.

The clerk sat at the desk, nodding, and Winston turned back without a sound. His suspicions of the man had mounted in recent days, and tonight, with Ellen gone and the knowledge that Braden's thin veneer of friendliness would vanish since she had irrevocably rejected him, his worry continued to center about Denton. He felt he must watch the clerk, and his mind raced over old, half-forgotten things that he had ignored before.

About midnight, satisfied with his watch on Denton, Cal Winston stole out the back door and into the dark alley. With the reassuring pressure of the gun on his hip, he walked to the alley's end where a side street ran north, then back to the other end. In the past, he remembered Braden's men had sometimes tied their horses behind the hotel; it might be, if they were coming in tonight, they would use the alley to avoid detection on Main Street. So he made several trips up and down. As the night advanced, the sky lightened and objects became clearer. Denton, as night clerk, was due to go off pretty soon, and Winston slipped back into the hotel to check again. Denton stood in the lobby near the door, looking out with no particular interest. Winston fixed his gaze on him for a full minute before returning to his vigil in the alley. As time dragged on he sensed the futility of waiting, and he made one last swing up and down his beat. He had cast a long look at the sky, estimating about two hours of night remained when from the northwest sounded the slow, muffled cadence of horses moving. At first he could not be certain, so he went to the alley's west end. Now he was certain. Looking north, he faced two horsemen coming toward him at a slow pace. He pulled out his gun, stepped back into the shadows to wait this out. The horses came on and instantly he caught something familiar about the lead rider. But he must be certain before he showed himself, so he waited with nervous impatience, the gun slippery in his hand from sweat.

The riders, instead of continuing down the street, swung into the alley's mouth. With his heart pounding, Winston stepped from the shadows, noticing the back horseman doubled over. Relief had its quick effect on the old man as he barred the way.

The front rider pulled up and cried out: "Dad!"

Winston said: "Let's get him inside, Ellen . . . quick . . . Denton's up front snooping around. We can use my room."

Together they lifted Durand down, Winston grunting with the heavy load. Through the back way they carried the wounded man, and, once Durand lay upon the bed, Winston quickly left the room and tiptoed down the hall. Denton was back at the desk, smoking and puttering with the nervousness of a bobcat.

Chapter Fourteen

Doc Gates lived in his cramped office over MacGregor's Mercantile store near the middle of Main Street, and Cal Winston found him stretched out asleep on a ragged old leather couch, snoring sonorously. The sour smell of whiskey hung heavily in the untidy room, which included two cane-bottom chairs, a rickety table loaded down with a pill bag, bottles, and a cluttered assortment of medicines. Against the far wall stood a ponderous bookcase filled with books, most of them volumes on treating gunshot wounds. Townsmen said of Gates that, when he wasn't drinking at the Osage Girl, he poured over the books. He accomplished both tasks efficiently.

Winston lighted the lamp and in the low, yellow flare stared down at the lean, disheveled figure with misgivings. Gates would wake up trembling, but maybe a couple of drinks would steady him. Wasn't the man a marvel with wounds, despite his weakness for the flowing cup? After several shakes, the angular, unkempt man on the couch stirred and mumbled: "What's this?"

Cal Winston told him. It took time for the words to sink in. Gates seemed to be weighing their meaning. Tiredly he said: "All right. But I'll need a drink for this night's business."

"There's a quart at the hotel. Come on."

He had to steady the doctor down the step, but, once in the alley, he took a grip on himself and began walking without wavering. They eased through the back entrance and into the room without raising a clamor. There Winston took the whiskey from a shelf and handed it silently to Gates, who took two long pulls in fast succession. "Ah!" he exclaimed, and an alertness and life sprang back into his thin face and he prepared to look at Walt Durand.

"Get some hot water," Gates told Ellen.

She darted for the door, but halted and turned to her father. "Denton," she said thoughtfully. "He'll know something's up when he sees me carrying water."

Winston said—"I'll take care of that."—and moved to the door. "You come up in five minutes."

On second thought he left the gun and holster behind, advanced into the lobby, yawning loudly, and stopped at the desk. "I'm up early this mornin', Denton. Still worried about Ellen. You knock off. I'll hold down here till the day man comes on."

Denton hesitated, his quick mind trying to see through this unusual change. Yet he guessed Ellen's absence explained it.

"Go on," Winston said easily, and he went around behind the desk with a positive manner that settled the matter. Denton went up to his room to wait for breakfast before getting his sleep. He alternated at day and night shifts. Lately, at Braden's urging, he had insisted to Cal Winston on taking the night watch. He lay down, a slight but wiry man with small, piercing eyes, sharp nose, and a quick, furtive manner. A precisely trimmed moustache hovered over his thin mouth. He began thinking about Braden, Red Cloud, and the people who made up its citizenry. He found nothing there but distaste and a longing to get away.

He was a city man, had spent most of his working years clerking in Kansas City hotels, and the change to the raw border town grated upon him as foreign, rough, and repulsive. He did not fit here and he knew it. Although he much preferred Kansas City, there was that little matter of money stolen from a hotel safe, entrusted to him. So, cornered, he had quietly packed his grip and eased out of town. Two days later he was in Dodge City. Since then he had drifted into Colorado mining towns, back to Kansas, and now this "border hole," as he described it. Flat broke, he had encountered Braden in a saloon; surprisingly the man had offered to help him. Within a short time he was clerking at the Western Star. Soon thereafter he learned why Braden has helped him. His real job was to watch Ellen and her father and report their movements. That proved easy and uneventful until Larry Cramer arrived and left, followed by Durand. Denton began to find his sleuthing wearing thin. Not that his conscience bothered him. Instead, it was the strong element of danger. And there was the intercepted letter from Durand to Cramer. Denton, in checking over the mail, had slipped it neatly in his coat, read it in his room, and turned it over to Braden. He knew the message had marked Cramer for death, and, as he expected, the man had not returned alive. The letter also told Braden when Durand was coming. However, remorse was not a part of Denton's being and he was without fear until the tall, hard figure of Durand appeared menacingly. That Durand and Winston might suspect him, he was aware, which kept a continual fear bubbling inside him. Thus Braden's hold grew upon him and Denton knew that he stood deeply involved. And this fear! Not even Matt Braden's power could erase that.

When Ellen came into the lobby, her father followed her though the darkened dining room into the kitchen where he kindled a fire. The woman helper would come at six o'clock to open the dining room. After waiting for the water to boil, Winston came out to the lobby and looked casually overhead. Nothing moved at the head of the stairway, so he nodded, and Ellen, carrying a boiling tea kettle and a roll of white cloth, came out and they hurried to the back room.

Doc Gates was setting the quart bottle back on the shelf when they entered. Unabashed, he rolled a cigarette with steadying hands and his faded eyes glinted. Winston marveled at him; only a few minutes before Gates could not have pulled on his boots without help. Now he had won full control of himself. He worked steadily on Durand and after a time announced with a touch of professional pride: "He'll make it easy with rest. Bullet went clean through him. Lost a river of blood but he's tough as one of Luke Givins's mules."

Gates picked up his shapeless hat. "I'll come back this evenin' for another look. He's my only patient, now that that Texas cowboy is up again. I'll leave him in your hands, Miss Ellen," he added with a strange courtliness.

Cal Winston stopped the doctor at the door. "We want to keep this quiet, Doc."

Gates straightened up with injured pride. "Don't insult me, Cal. I still retain a few ethics of my profession. Why, I know enough to hang every outlaw in the Territory, only there ain't enough rope for 'em all."

"I didn't mean that," Winston answered with an impatient wave of his hand. "Have a drink before you leave."

The doctor's face relaxed and he smiled. "I'd be delighted. It's far better'n that red-eye I had last night."

Ellen slept in a rocker until noon. When she awakened and went over to the bed, Durand opened his eyes. Through his blanketing weariness he noted distantly the gladness and relief in her eyes. He said something, but the low words failed to carry to her. She bent closer over the bearded face. He said again: "So we made it."

She fed him later. Her father came in and out several times. With Durand sleeping late in the afternoon, she fell asleep in the rocker again.

Once, her father opened the door, saw them sleeping, and closed the door without speaking.

A low light glimmered in the room as Durand opened his eyes again. Ellen sat before him, watching the door. She had freshened up and he noticed the flush on her cheeks, the brightness in her eyes. She didn't look like a woman who had just retrieved a wounded man from the hills. Her range garb had been replaced with a fresh print dress, which clung to her, marking her graceful outline. He watched her with a silent hunger in his eyes until he fell asleep again.

She turned her eyes upon him, letting her thoughts wander. In the stillness here, the ordeal of finding him and bringing him back seemed unreal, that is until she remembered Braden. Her father said not a Braden man had been in town since she had brought Durand in. That had its comfort, but it held out the sharp possibility of real danger. What would happen when Braden and Kane rode into town? They would not suspect that Durand was here. Yet there was the quick-eyed Denton. Braden's abrupt change, since he had learned how he stood with her, had surprised her in one way, and in another it had not. She would not admit it to herself at first, but through his deliberate courtship, his stiff and correct manner toward her, and his smoothness, she had found a hardness a less alert woman would not have detected. Until Walt Durand came to Red Cloud, there had been no other man who visited her regularly, although she had danced and ridden with the younger cowboys. Somehow word had got around that she was Braden's girl, which tended to fend off any anxious suitors. He was a big man, important through a country whose life strings all knotted up at Red Cloud. At first his attention had not been unpleasant, but that had gradually worn off. Early in his courtship she discovered she had no feeling for the man, and, by the time Durand came, she had fully decided what she would tell Braden when he asked her. He, too, must have known that she had no warmth for him, that they were far apart. His stubbornness and driving power to seize what he wanted pushed him on hopefully, thinly veiling what he really knew. And now, what he could not have, he would seek to destroy; her knowledge of Matt Braden told her that, and her fear of him rose.

That fear raced through her when there came a slight scraping sound in the hallway. Her father had hung Durand's holster against the wall, and she slipped the heavy gun in one hand and faced the door. Next she heard her father call her name softly; the door opened, and her fear vanished. Wyatt was with him, and the Texan took off his hat awkwardly, nodded silently to her, and stood looking down at Durand.

"How's he makin' it?" Wyatt inquired.

"Slow, but he's going to be all right."

Wyatt's long blond hair hung loosely, his big-boned body stood out strongly, overshadowing all else in the room. "Reckon he's safe here?" Wyatt asked.

"Safe as anywhere right now," Winston told him.

Wyatt's set face showed his concern. "There'll be hell to pay when Braden's men hit town. They'll come smokin'. But my boys are primed and waitin'."

"Doc Gates is late," Ellen said with irritation.

"Wonder what's keeping him."

"He's probably wooin' the Osage Girl again," her father said. "Guess I'll have to run him down. I'm beginnin' to feel like a hound dog, the way I have to tail that man."

"I'll play hound dog with you," Wyatt broke in, and they left together.

For some time Ellen sat in the rocker, watching Durand, thinking. This helpless waiting for Braden to make his inevitable move had its wearing effect on her, and now footsteps sounded in the hallway. She stood up straight and nerve-bound. The noise ceased, as if the walker might be listening. Breathing faster, she opened the door and looked out. A man, a little man, stood at the far end where the lobby's light showed. Closing the door behind her, she went boldly down there, making no attempt to walk softly. It was Denton, of course. He gave her his cool, shifting smile, which revealed his small, pointed, yellow teeth; he made no move to retire to the lobby.

"What do you want?" she demanded.

"Nothing . . . just looking for your father."

His unctuous manner toward her reminded her of a snake; it did not ring true; it was something that marked him from range men. She looked at him, hard and straightforward, and said: "He'll be back soon enough. I'll tell him."

"Thank you, Miss Ellen," he said, and turned back, leaving behind him a half-mocking impression that angered her. After entering the lobby, Denton perched on his high stool behind the desk, thinking: *Damned funny she came out of that room so fast. This whole damned place is waiting for something to happen. I can feel it.* He would have to pass the word to Braden and Kane. What he wanted now was enough money to leave this hole, and he might manage that if he knew enough.

By nine o'clock Denton could no longer stay behind the desk. He had always been nervous and high strung, so his unrest drove him out to the verandah. Down the street, lights from the saloons shot out slender, probing fingers; elsewhere the town squatted drowsily under a clear moon, wrapped up for the night. He spat disgustedly over the railing into the thick dust. Now in Kansas City events would just be warming up. How he'd like to stroll into a hotel—a real hotel—nattily dressed, with a free-and-easy girl on his arm, money in his pocket. Money, that's what he had to have, and Braden represented his sole hope in that respect.

From far out on the virgin prairie the wind carried to him a coyote's mournful howl; it made him cold, a bit fearful; he had heard those howls every night here, but he'd never gotten used to them. He was a city man, a Kansas City man. How was he going to get out of Red Cloud? That thought kept hammering in his head without solution, and he was frowning on that problem when he noticed two men come down Main Street to the hotel corner, where they turned off north. It struck him as odd for this time of night, and, with sudden interest pricking him, he walked fast to the corner and looked after them.

Nothing stirred in the shadows. So, keeping close to the wall on his left, he stole up to the alley and looked into it. Two men were stepping into the rear entrance of the hotel, and, as light sketched them, he recognized the shuffling, bent figure of Doc Gates and the heavy-set person of Cal Winston. They moved in quickly and the light shut off, as if a door had been closed.

With a start, Denton saw that his position would be precarious if caught snooping and he raced back to the hotel corner. In long, cat-like steps he gained the verandah, puffing from the short run, but trying to look casual if Winston came out. His luck was good. A glance revealed the empty lobby. To further his rôle of casualness, he rolled a cigarette and stayed outside a few minutes. His heart had stopped pounding when he came in; he dared not look again into the hall, but it didn't matter much just now. He had stumbled onto something tonight; something was going on back there. Smirking to himself, he took his place at the desk with a rich, quickening feeling of triumph. He was bent over the register, apparently studying it, when Winston appeared from the hall.

"Nice evening, Mister Winston," said Denton cheerfully.
"Yes, 'tis."

What is eating the man? Winston asked himself. *Only this evening he has been openly sullen and surly at times. Why this sudden change of humor?* Looking into the clerk's pale, hard face, he saw nothing there but the bland, disarming-designed smile, which hid whatever he thought. Winton didn't linger long. This was no time for foolish, time-killing talk with Denton. A disturbing perception had warned Winston, something he'd discovered from behind that too ready smile and manner. As easy and naturally as he could then, he bent his heavy steps back to the sick room. . . .

Along toward eleven o'clock the wind whipped up out of the southeast, slapping and banging Main Street's over-hanging boardwalk signs and propelling dusty gusts against the weather-grayed buildings. And this wind wrought a change in Denton, dispelling his elation; to him, its beat and moan was a grim reminder of his isolation, coldly reëmphasizing the harsh fact that he stood alone as a stranger, without friends and money in this raw, rough land. Now he was counting on his message to Braden to harvest sufficient funds for passage out of town on the stage, and, if Braden failed to come through, damned if he wouldn't get out anyway. Self-pity had its way with him, and again he hated everything connected with Red Cloud.

Suddenly his far-away mental meandering was broken. Above the lonesome ramblings of the wind crept a low throbbing and drumming; it stayed constant, rolling up out of the prairie vastness like distant thunder, now fanning out into a distinct pounding. Horses, many of them, were coming. It wasn't long until hoofs crashed hard upon the street, hammered to the hotel, and stopped. It had to be Braden; it was Braden. He jangled into the lobby, dusty-booted and unshaven, his generally meticulous trappings travel-grimed. Red Kane loomed up behind him and riders spilled through the doorway.

"Up there," Braden said evenly, waving men upstairs as he faced Denton.

The clerk didn't move; he was afraid again. He wanted to sink down and away from Braden's fire-eyed glare. Never had he seen the range king like this. Gone was his smoothness, stripped by a driving, undeniable force reflected in his broad face and body and thin mouth.

"Where they hidin'?" Braden snapped. "Found their camp in the hills. They've got to be in Red Cloud."

Denton, puzzled, gestured with a thumb. "Back there . . . the girl and the old man."

Braden's anger leaped out. "To hell with them! I want Durand!"

Sweat beaded Denton's forehead; his mouth sagged open. "Durand? I ain't seen him. But Doc Gates and Winston came in the back way couple of hours ago."

That was enough for Braden. Flinging Denton a look of scorn and triumph, he bulled his way down the hall, his men following in a pack while others searched upstairs. He didn't pause to knock at the back room; the door was unlocked and he jerked it open.

Ellen Winston rose from a chair to meet him face to face, her wide eyes startled but cool.

He looked for fear, but found none, which surprised him. "I want Durand," he intoned. "Where you hidin' him?"

"Your manners are bad tonight, Matt."

He couldn't miss the taunt and mockery in her eyes. "You didn't answer my question, so we're comin' in."

And Braden went in, with Kane behind him, pushing her aside with one arm. Braden's eyes swept the room—roved to the empty bed. He glared at Ellen and snapped at Kane: "Look in that closet, Red."

Red Kane's meat-red face grinned its pleasure as he fingered his gun and tore back the curtain. He rustled among the clothes hanging in there, found nothing, and looked at his boss with disappointment.

The woman's cool voice hit Braden again as his gaze played back on the empty bed. "What did you expect to find, Matt?"

His wrath came out again, and he said: "That's a fool question, because you know what I'm lookin' for. Now where is he?"

He was trying to jolt her into anger in the hope she might give away something, for he knew he couldn't scare her now, but her voice held its level, sustained tone.

"If I knew, I wouldn't tell you. Go ahead and search the hotel if that'll satisfy you."

Braden smiled. "We're doin' that little chore right now."

More men clumped in the hallway and a man with a face the shade of saddle leather came in and announced: "Nothin' upstairs."

Braden shrugged his shoulders. "There are other places to look. Clear out now." He stayed behind the others, still watching Ellen. He wanted to hurt her, and he said: "You'll hate the day you took up with that killer."

He stressed the last word, which fanned a flame to her face. Coldly she asked: "And why will I be sorry?"

"Because I'm going to kill Durand . . . shoot him down like he did my men!"

Chapter Fifteen

That Matt Braden planned to stick in town until he flushed Walt Durand from hiding was all too apparent. The broad chieftain's riders made the Osage Girl their powwow grounds and boycotted Luke Givins's barn, stalling their mounts at a livery in the west end operated by a close-mouthed character named Fremont who had connections in the Territory and was not particular about his patrons, so long as they paid him. In return, he kept his mouth shut.

Red Kane issued the edict to the crew. "We won't trade with any friend of Durand's," he ordered.

Most of the townsmen, aware of the powder-keg situation, wisely kept their opinions to themselves, all except Andrew MacGregor, the merchant who openly championed Durand. "He's the first man," MacGregor said, "with the guts to stand up to Matt Braden. I take off my hat to him and may the Lord throw a gun on his side."

Speculation as to Durand's hide-out provided the town with its choice gossip. If he was in town, he was exceptionally well hidden, for Red Cloud's size did not lend itself to hide-outs. None of the townsmen knew for sure and it didn't matter anyway, because they were going to let Matt Braden do all the searching.

Red Kane's addiction to poker kept him inside much of the time; nevertheless he and Braden held several councils of war daily. They sent horsemen ranging through the hills and at night posted men along the streets. "Somebody will slip," Braden predicted, "then we'll smoke him out."

Now Doc Gates also discovered that his peaceful days were to be interrupted. No threats or violence were flung at him, yet, when he left the saloon or his office, men tailed him at a distance and he thought of the caged squirrel he had had as a boy back in Missouri. His reaction was to ignore the watchers and down his daily quota of red-eye with unvarying frequency.

The next day after Braden searched the hotel, Ellen Winston went about her routine chores in the dining room. Twice, during the afternoon, her father whispered messages to her, and that night she threw a shawl over her shoulders and went boldly out the front way with Denton staring after her. At the first street east, she turned north, cut west behind the Western Star, then continued north until she neared the town's edge. The wild smell of the prairie swarmed over her pleasantly as she looked about to see if she was being followed. She decided she was not and walked eastward, moving within the slanting shadow images of buildings when she could. Directly north of Givins's stable, she drew up against a feed shed to look again. Horses moved in the big corral behind the stable, otherwise this section of town lay fixed in its night bivouac. She started for the street, planning to make her crossing here between the barn and Lane's saddle shop, which lay across a wide open space to the west from the stable. Halfway to the street, she veered for the saddle shop's wall and was within a rope's throw of stepping out to cross the street when a man's slouching figure on the other side checked her. Pressing against the wall, she expected him to stride across to her. She had feared just this—that afternoon she had been watched as she went about the stores making her purchases for the dining room. And now. . . .

The man paced eastward a few steps and cast a long, searching glance at the stable and the road that snaked out toward Elgin, and, as if he were patrolling a beat, he turned and strolled back in the direction of the saloons. When his back blurred out up the street, she ran across the dust-bedded stretch to a point between two low buildings. She wanted to continue running, but forced herself to walk. Looking back once again, she hurried resolutely on until a frame building, circled by a neat fence, was before her. She remembered that a bell always tinkled when you opened the weight-hung gate, so she silenced the tiny clapper with one hand while she opened the gate with the other. A dull light peeped from the front part of the house. She rapped softly but insistently at the door. Her answer was Martha Givins unlocking and opening it and shutting it swiftly behind her.

They talked then in short, excited whispers.

Ellen asked first: "How is he? I couldn't get here sooner. They're watching all of us."

"I know, I know." Then: "Why, he's doing fine as could be. Hungry all the time . . . which is a good sign. Only he wants to get away, says he can't stay here and bring Matt Braden's wrath down on us. He'll be riding out of here soon, Ellen, or I don't know men of his like. I begged him to stay . . . told him we didn't owe Braden anything. But Walt Durand has his own strict code . . . he don't want other people to fend for him. Sometimes I wonder about him. When he sleeps, that brown face of his gets younger . . . like a boy's. Reminds me of a boy Luke and I had once. . . ." Martha's soft voice dropped huskily; it was throaty and remembering and a little sad. "This afternoon I noticed him look out the window where the prairie stretches out, and I swear I never saw a man look the way he did. His eyes was real piercin'-like, like he could see things I couldn't, over and beyond the hills. And he was lonesome, I could see that. I know he's a good man, Ellen. Maybe he has killed some men, but they needed killin' or he wouldn't have done it. It takes men like him to make a country good and clean, fit for women and children. He's been through hard times, I can see that. But he never talks about himself, never mentions a gun. Why, he hadn't been here any time before he had me tellin' him all about Luke and me and our boy who died in Colorado. Oh, I just know he's a good man."

Martha put her arms around the younger woman and hugged her close, and Ellen felt her tremble.

"You're worn out, Martha. Get some sleep. I'll stay until near daylight."

While coffee warmed on the stove, Ellen turned over in her mind Mrs. Givins's words about Durand. They had struck her powerfully, arousing deep-seated emotions that quickened her breathing and blotted out, for the moment, all the ugly, pressing fears of recent days. It was a kind of delicious feeling of overwhelming happiness, newly found and disturbing and sweet and wistful.

Durand slept in a darkened back room off the kitchen, and, after Martha left to get some sleep, Ellen went in to see him. First, however, she took a lamp to the door to look at him briefly, mentally noting that he needed shaving and that she must remind her father to do that tomorrow. With the lamp out, she sat near him, listening to his heavy breathing. Durand was still sleeping when, later, Ellen entered Martha's room and aroused her.

For three days, Ellen had made late night trips to the Givins' home, taking a different course each time. It seemed to her that the men who stalked her had relaxed their vigilance—that, in fact, her journeys were becoming too easy. That made her more wary than before, but no one stopped her and tension within the town lost its sharp edge and a fair degree of normalcy returned.

One afternoon there came a knock at her door as she lay

159

napping. Denton stood outside at a respectable distance. He said: "Matt Braden wants to see you. He's out in the lobby."

She hesitated, wondering what he could want. "Tell him I'll see him." She didn't want to meet him here in her room. She wanted the meeting to be out in the open, and perhaps she could learn something.

Standing grandiosely in the lobby, Braden's demeanor and appearance were in striking contrast to the night he had searched the hotel, when he looked even rougher than his men. He held a cream-colored sombrero in one hand, his fancy, hand-tooled boots glistened, and he wore a spotless gray shirt to match the finely tailored trousers you couldn't buy in Red Cloud. Topping off that was a bright-colored scarf, tied short at the collar like a tie.

"Let's go for a ride," he began with a disarming smile, speaking as he had in the old days.

"If you have anything to say, you can say it here." What did he expect her to do, fawn on him like one of the women at the Osage Girl?

She might as well have spoken a warm greeting for the effect it had on him. "I want to get myself straight about the other night," he said coolly and easily. "This fight's between me and Durand, not you. I don't hold anything against you or your dad. It's Durand . . . he stole my horses, killed my men. Now it's him or me. That's the way I look at it . . . the way any man would."

"Don't make excuses for yourself, Matt. They don't hold water and you know it."

She had already wearied of this talk. His colossal ego was even greater than she imagined; it angered and amazed her.

"I'd even call this off, Ellen, if you. . . ."

She whirled away, her temper running flush through her cheeks.

Braden did not finish what he had to say, although it was plain enough what he meant. At that moment, from the open dining room door, sounded a bellow of rage and Cal Winston came out with the old revolver held threateningly in one gnarled hand.

"Get out, Braden!" the old man cried, coming forward. The gun pointed straight at the cowman's belt line and there was no mistaking the ringing menace in the command.

But Braden didn't budge.

"Get out!" rang the command again.

"Now don't get jerky with that trigger finger, Cal. Can't Ellen and I have a talk? Why, Cal, this is the first time I ever knew you to throw down on a man. Didn't know you carried one of those cannons." He was trying to soothe the old man, but Winston stubbornly trained the gun on Braden's middle.

"Now that you know I carry a gun, wheel on out of here! Anything you'd want to say ain't worth listenin' to."

"You're makin' it hard on yourself, Cal."

"That's my business, my worry."

Braden grinned darkly. "I could pass the word along that the Western Star no longer welcomes any guests . . . that it might be unhealthy for any man to tie up here."

"Braden," warned Winston, "you got five seconds to get through that door. Take your choice. One . . . two. . . ."

On the count of four Braden turned and went to the door. One blazing look and he was gone down the steps. He knew that Cal Winston would shoot. Over the years he had learned the subtle shade of difference between bluff and determination. Old Cal wasn't bluffing. As he walked heavily back to the Osage Girl, he wasn't exactly a surprised man. He had known, back in his mind, that Ellen would not change her attitude. In his stubborn, rugged way of thinking, he hated to give up the fight for her, although he knew it was lost. She was the only woman he had ever wanted for keeps. Now that loss burned him deeply; he would see to it that Durand never got her, even if she wanted him.

Cal Winston slipped the gun back in his holster. There was a wooden look on his old face, although it showed no fear, and, too, there was a touch of embarrassment over the gun. Ellen hadn't seen him with a gun in his hand since she was a little girl in the Dakotas.

Ellen took him by the arm. "You took a big chance. But I'm proud of you. Who said you couldn't stand up to the tough ones?"

He smiled wearily. "I'm just out of practice. I'd have shot him, though. We don't have to take anything from Braden or any other range rooster," he growled. "But," he went on heavily, "our days in Red Cloud are numbered. Braden will find some way to break us. Better pack your things. We'll have to get out before long,"

"But you just said we wouldn't back down. That's quitting!"

Some of the old fury came back to him. Her words had struck a soft spot—his pride. He raised his head and said: "Maybe you're right, Ellen. Your mother. . . ."

"Let's stick it out."

"All right . . . for a while. I'm thinkin' of you, not myself."

Movement behind the desk caught their attention. Denton, who had been behind the desk all this time, was noisily turning the register's pages.

Cal Winston took a big breath then and crossed over. "Denton," he said distinctly, "you seem to like Braden's clan, so git out and git your belly full of him. There's a stage in here at three o' clock. If you ain't on it when it pulls out, don't come snoopin' back here. Else I'll trim that little black brush under your nose with a Forty-Five slug."

The clerk's small eyes narrowed suddenly. "What have I done?" His voice was shaking, and he was scared again.

"You did a good job spyin' for Braden."

Denton's mouth formed a protest, but he saw the futility of it with the big blue barrel of the gun in his face. Beaten, he went upstairs to pack his things without saying another word.

"Might as well run all the rats out the same day," old Cal told his daughter. "Now I'm gonna watch that stage. If he don't catch it, he'll wish he had."

"Getting him away from the hotel is enough, isn't it?" she asked.

"No, it ain't," he said defiantly, and she knew that settled it.

The stage for Elgin rattled into town shortly before three o'clock and stopped in front of the express office next to Lane's saddle shop. Cal Winston waited out in front. As two passengers got out, glad the rocketing ride was over, Winston looked about him for Denton. The clerk was not to be found. Cal looked once more toward the hotel, then he saw Denton coming along the boardwalk, carrying two suitcases. When the clerk came up, Winston met him and paid him off, keeping the old gun handy, just in case.

"You ready?" asked Winston.

"Ready as I'll ever be," answered Denton, and he stepped up to the stage and inside.

Six fresh horses were brought up from Luke Givins's stable and hitched to the stage. Cal Winston stood near the stage door, looking at Denton. "You ain't a cow town man, anyway," Winston said. "There's a hotel in Elgin . . . try that."

The traces tightened as the driver on the box called out and cracked his whip. The stage jerked and went reeling off down the street with the big wheels spinning dust.

Denton, the lone passenger this trip, looked out at the prairie with surging elation. He was thinking of another place, a town called Kansas City, and the empty safe back at the Western Star. . . .

After night settled down, Ellen Winston went to the Givins' home again. Durand was up and restless, sitting in a rocking chair. Martha Givins left them and Ellen told him about Denton.

"I was surprised at Dad," she said. "I didn't know he had it in him to get rough."

"I'm not. Your dad knows when he's pushed far enough. That's easy to see."

She said thoughtfully: "It shows what will happen sooner or later. Walt, I'm afraid they'll find you. They're watching everywhere . . . men walking the streets, riders constantly snooping. It's like a military encampment. I've had to dodge men every night, and if they start searching the houses. . . ."

"I ought to get out of here," Durand said heavily. "I'm placing the burden on my friends. Braden could break any one of them for helping me. Look at your dad. They'll ruin him. Tomorrow night I aim to ride out of here. I've made up my mind."

"But you can hardly sit in that chair."

"I can stick on a horse."

"That isn't enough. Where would you go?"

Durand looked at her searchingly. "Haven't thought that far ahead. To Fort Reno, I guess. The main thing is to leave here, so none of you folks will get hurt. Naturally I'll have to come back and finish the job."

"Oh, Walt, there must be a better way than that. You can't ride yet."

"Tell Jim Wyatt to get me a horse ready."

"Take me with you!" She was leaning toward him, almost pleading, and he caught her pleasant nearness, and he half rose then and she moved to him and he was holding her. As he kissed her with a violence that forced her head back, she held to him as the room and its dim light and all that troubled them was swept away in a giddy whirlpool in which only they stood clear and dominant

Footsteps from the front part of the house separated them, and Luke and Martha came in with Doc Gates.

"Get ready to ride, Durand!" Luke said warningly.

"What's up?" But Walt Durand figured he knew without asking.

"Tell him, Doc."

Doc Gates, visibly excited, tried to talk but the words wouldn't come out. He spluttered and gasped. He had been running and the unaccustomed physical work had exhausted him.

"Find him a drink, Mother," said Luke.

Martha found the whiskey and Gates reached for it desperately. The raw liquor made a rumbling, gulping noise as it went down, but the doctor could talk now. "It's Braden," he said nervously. "I was having a drink at the Osage Girl when I heard a rider say something about Luke's house, that maybe they'd better search it since Durand wasn't anywhere else. They've been through my barn a couple of times. When this rider went back to talk with Braden and Kane, I slipped out and ran down here. That's all I know, but they'll be down here."

"I'll wrangle a fast hoss from the barn for you," Luke said.

As he turned to rush out, Ellen said: "Saddle two, Luke. I'm going with him."

"What! Ellen, you can't. . . ."

Durand joined Luke in voicing his disapproval, but Ellen turned with pleading words to Martha, certain of her support. "He'll need someone to help him, Martha. You can understand."

And mild-mannered Martha Givins rapped back stoutly: "Yes, I can. Now, Luke, you run down to the barn for two horses. Ellen can help me get some things together. Hurry!"

While the women made up a blanket pack of food and clothing, Durand buckled on his heavy gun belt and Gates helped himself to another drink from the bottle. This scene, this urgency, had its thrill for Durand, for she was going with him.

They were ready and waiting when Luke brought the horses around to the back of the house. The night was an inky mask and the wind was rising. Before they mounted, Luke told Ellen: "Go to that old line rider's cabin at Cottonwood Springs. Wait there till you hear from Jim Wyatt. He's waiting for you now at the edge of town near the barn."

Luke and Gates helped Durand into his saddle. Durand felt little slivers of pain shoot through the wound, but they eased off as he settled down in the saddle.

They mumbled good byes, and then they rode off, northeast, from the house, lost at once in the darkness.

Back in the house, Martha Givins said jerkily: "Let's clean up this place. If Braden comes, he won't find what he wants."

Luke looked at her sharply. "Why, Mother," he said, "you're crying."

"Luke Givins," she said defensively, no longer trying to hide her weeping, "shut up and help me clean this house."

Durand and Ellen stopped. Horses moved heavily somewhere ahead of them along Main Street. When it was quiet again, they rode until they sighted the broad outline of the barn. From out of the shadows of a low building rose a man.

Jim Wyatt's drawling voice met them. "Can you hang on that hoss for a few hours, Durand?"

"Reckon I can. I'll have to."

"Go on now," Wyatt said urgently, "an' don't stop."

Hoofs *thudded* menacingly down the street. Wyatt whirled. "Pull out, Durand," he warned. "Keep movin'."

The Texan, looming, tall and formidable, left them abruptly and went straight west along the street. In his terse command urging them to ride off, Durand was impressed by the finality in the friendly tone. Durand hesitated.

Ellen's voice reached out anxiously: "Hurry, Walt!"

Jim Wyatt was lost in the street's black core. Ellen called again and Durand kicked his horse out and they rode off eastward. Hardly 100 yards from the barn, they heard the *clatter* of a running horse break out behind them. It was followed by a single blast from a gun, then another and another, close together. Now the horse wasn't running any more. . . .

Chapter Sixteen

Piano music tinkled like the soft patter of gently falling broken glass as a little man labored over the keys, pounding out a foot-moving tune fresh from Dodge City's roaring dance halls and deadfalls. Couples danced strenuously through the haze of blue smoke flooding the bar and floor of the sprightly Osage Girl, the Braden's crew's hang-out.

A red-eyed peeler from the Territory, made mellow and affable by the establishment's high-voltage whiskey, braced his elbows against the bar, highly pleased with the little piano player's production.

"He shore can paw the ivories, can't he?" said the red-eyed man, addressing no one in particular.

The saloon was filling up rapidly as its regular clientele, augmented by Matt Braden's many riders, checked in for the evening. Every night had been like this since Braden's bunch had taken over the town. They spent money freely, gave the girls upstairs a strong play, and there apparently was an inexhaustible supply of whiskey on hand. Barkeeps smiled as they poured out a steady river of drinks and listened to the constant murmurings of the crowd, the steady rhythm of the tireless music-maker in the rear, the high-flung laughter of women, and the *clink* of coins from the gaming tables. The fact that this sudden prosperity was due to the riders' search for a single man, and that they would shoot him down like a coyote once they found him, in no way deterred the bright ardor of the slick-haired men doling out drinks from behind the bar. These manhunts, they recalled without labor, had occurred before and the results had always been the same—Braden's men spent their money, ran down their quarry, and rode back to their hill country. You had to get the money when you could in the saloon business and never mind from where it came. It was the same way with the girls upstairs. And Braden's boys always had money. And no telling when some cowpuncher would shoot up the place and splinter the big mirror behind the bar. And getting in glassware from Ark City was a long haul. Sometimes you had to go farther than that.

Matt Braden and Red Kane, coming out of the little powwow room at the rear, eyed the dancers disgustedly. Over at the bar, on which Doc Gates said he knew every scratch, half a dozen bearded Braden men lounged and watched indolently. The sight of women, even painted women, was pleasing to a man who ate sowbelly, beans, and gravy and drank black coffee three times every day and washed in a creek once a month.

"Look at that," Kane growled, slanting his head at the dancers.

"No wonder Durand's still free as a buck Injun. You can't chase the calico and catch a man."

"You're the foreman," Braden reminded him. "Roost 'em out. Do something about it."

"I'll do just that."

Kane signaled with his hand and Cash Edmund came over from the bar, his deadpan, wind-beaten face almost solemn and grave.

"Holin' up here early tonight, ain't they?" Kane questioned. "I told you to keep them out, to watch the town. Durand's still loose, an' whatever we catch, it won't be in this place."

Cash Edmund obeyed orders to the letter, but he disliked taking them, and Kane's manner of giving them now rubbed him the wrong way. "Hell, we just got in!" he replied testily, shifting his small frame directly in front of the broad-beamed foreman. "We've rode this moss-horned hole of a town till we're plumb saddle sore. If Durand's here, he's keepin' company with a prairie dog. My eyesight ain't that sharp."

"Still checkin' the hotel?"

"Sure. Two men down there now. Not a shadow reported yet."

Kane went on insistently. "Who's at the stable? That's where he'd have to wrangle a hoss. If he's still alive . . . an' I believe he is . . . he'll make a break to a hoss."

"Shelton's watchin' the stable," Edmund said. "Just came in . . . over at the bar now."

Shelton, his back to the crowd, was talking earnestly to a rider on his right. On his other side, Doc Gates leaned in a familiar pose, challenging a full glass of whiskey that squatted tantalizingly on the moist, polished bar. Braden's roving eyes gave Gates a long, piercing inspection as Edmund and Shelton *jangled* forward. Braden was thinking: *That damned sawbones must have doctored Durand, an' knows where he is.* If nothing else, Braden speculated, he could make Gates talk.

A tall, bony man with thin shoulders and enormously long arms, Shelton weaved a little and his eyes had a bleary, bloodshot cast. Like the others with whom he rode, with the exception of Braden, Kane, and Edmund, he had kept the bartenders bending their elbows; also like the others, he made a better hand away from town, when he was assigned a definite job that kept him riding long before sunup until long after sundown.

Braden took up the questioning this time. "Scared up anything tonight?" he asked Shelton.

Shelton shook his head negatively. He didn't much give a damn the way he felt tonight. "Not much . . . just old Givins, comin' in an' out by his lonesome. Nobody took out a horse."

Braden's alert mind weighed this report. "Where'd he go? What'd he do? Anybody with him?"

"One time Doc Gates came down to the stable. They went in the back for a while, then Doc came out an' went uptown."

"When was that?"

"About dark."

"What about Luke Givins? He stay at the barn?"

"He made a couple of trips to his house. I just remarked to one of the boys at the bar. . . ."

Braden's cold eyes seemed to burn through Shelton with sudden understanding. "That's it!" he exclaimed.

Men at nearby poker tables turned and the *clink* of chips ceased as Braden almost shouted the words.

"See it now, Red?" said Braden in singing triumph. "Givins's house . . . they've got Durand there maybe. We're gonna look that place over. Why didn't we think of that before?" Braden's quick gaze switched to the bar. "Doc Gates figures in this," he said. "Now where in hell did he go?" Braden kept peering along the bar, up and down at its patrons. All that marked Doc Gates's position was the now empty whiskey glass.

"He took off," Kane grunted vacantly. "But we can run him down. He can't stay away from a saloon long enough to hide out."

Word spread to Braden's other crew members, and men began vacating the bar and tables, spilling out to the tie rack. Some left their cards reluctantly. Braden, always the leader, hit the saddle first and a dozen men swung in behind him at a fast trot as they moved out like a cavalry column. It wasn't necessary for anyone to show the way to Luke Givins's house; everyone knew where the man lived who ran the top livery stable. It was a little cottage sort of place, fashioned after a house Luke and Martha once lived in at Denver, different from the average Red Cloud house.

Luke Givins was in the act of taking the lamp into their neat bedroom when he first heard the horses drumming toward the house. Martha, cleaning up in the kitchen, heard them, too. She came running in to him.

"Could they be coming back?" she asked fearfully.

"No," Luke said. Those horses meant something more fearful than that. The base of the lamp grew slippery from sweat in his rough hand. "No, Mother," he said, listening. "It's somebody else. I think I know who. Durand and Ellen wouldn't come back here. Now you go in the bedroom and wait. Nobody's goin' to bother us."

"I will not!" she said stubbornly, and stuck beside him. "If it's Matt Braden, I'll run him out with a broom." Her voice quivered and Luke knew Martha was scared.

They heard horses come up to the front yard and behind the house. Then the front gate was opened noisily, spurs made their tinkling cadence and boots *thumped* hard upon the porch. Luke didn't wait for the command to open up. He knew it was coming, so he went to the door and opened it casually, as if he were expecting a neighbor. Red Kane's rough face greeted him.

"We're comin' in," growled Kane, and he came inside, other men pressing in behind him. At the same time the kitchen door was kicked open, and armed men poured inside and began going through the back rooms.

A deep-throated voice asked: "Where in hell is he?"

Luke had set the lamp down on a table, and, as calmly as if he were speaking to a friend, he asked: "Just what're you boys after?"

The intruders shuffled awkwardly. Breaking into the intimacy of a man's house was new to most of them, an act that, in a way, had its uneasy feeling of intrusion. They ignored

Luke and went on searching. Martha started to speak out, but Luke shushed her. "Now what is it?" he asked again, his words ringing evenly through the house. From his steady tone he might have been reprimanding a group of unruly boys.

From the kitchen Matt Braden, broad-beamed and confident, came forward into the crowded little front room. "That's a foolish question, Luke," he countered, "since you know what we're after."

Luke's jaw was set. "Can't say that I do," he said.

At first Braden had spoken with an oily, sarcastic smoothness. Now he cracked down, like a man bearing down on the first blow with a whip. "Where's Durand? He's been here. I found bandages in that back bedroom. You can't lie out of that."

Luke's stomach began tightening into a hard ball. He hadn't felt a tenseness like this since he'd carried a shotgun on the Denver stage and there'd been trouble at Cherry Creek. Braden wasn't fooling now, he knew. The man had dropped all pretense, which bared him as cold and unremitting. *Those bandages. . . .* Martha had told him to be sure and take them out, and, in his hurry and preoccupation, he had forgotten them. Luke waited, trying to fathom Braden, to wait him out, to turn aside those blazing eyes.

"I'm waitin' on you, Luke," said Braden. "But not long. You'd better talk."

Luke straightened up a bit, his eyes roving over the tense, friendless circle hemming him in. His head was clear; he sucked in a short gulp of air and plunged ahead, keeping his voice steady. "No reason for you to get anxious, Braden. I can't help you. You and Kane don't see things in the same light."

Braden smiled. "The bandages tell their own story.

What's your answer to that?"

"I can't help you."

"Quit stallin'."

Luke knew he was cornered. All he could do was try to ride this out, to weather Braden's fury.

"The bandages, Luke . . . the bandages," persisted Braden. "I won't wait forever."

Sweat beaded Luke's forehead like fine spray. The silence in the room assailed him. Conscious of Martha's drawn face, Luke said: "You'll have to figure it out for yourself."

Luke's answer came instantly. Braden lunged forward and one great hand rose and fell like a hammer, and Luke was the anvil as he fell to the floor like a felled steer. Martha cried out at the flat, meaty sound of fist against flesh and bent over her husband to protect him. Braden got in one vicious kick before Martha could cover Luke, and, as she looked up and saw Braden poised for another kick, she suddenly rose and lashed out at him futilely with her hands, scratching and pounding. Surprised, Braden fell back momentarily, then grasped her arms; she wilted in the unusual struggle, but, for the time, she had saved Luke additional battering. Braden flung her to one side when men stirred at the door, speaking out coarsely, and then Doc Gates was pushed roughly inside, jerking Braden's attention from the prostrate Luke.

"Caught him snoopin'," a man explained.

Without speaking, Braden appeared to lose control of himself. First, Red Kane, enjoying this little by-play like a gaunt prairie wolf hamstringing a weak-legged calf, grabbed Doc Gates by his bent shoulders and spun him like a top into Braden's hands. The doctor's eyes held their normally dull and bleary tint and he was obviously spent from the rough handling he had received. Instead of weakening, however, he glared up at Braden with surprising violence and fearless contempt, and it was that look, partly akin to the stubbornness Luke Givins had demonstrated, that set Braden off, kindling his wrath to a blazing pitch and purpling his face and steeling his eyes. This broken hulk of a man, physically weak and drink-sodden as he was, had, with old Givins, outmaneuvered all the gunmen who rode under the wide Braden banner—these thoughts burned their way through Braden.

Doc Gates expected the blows, but he was poorly prepared for their shaking violence. With one ham-like hand, the cattle chieftain smashed Gates's slack face; the blow knocked him back into the closely packed men. Kane smiled his rich pleasure at this, jerked the limp doctor up, and shoved him back at the waiting Braden, who smashed him down again with still greater violence. Gates was like a slender sapling before a woodsman's biting axe; his face shone raw and red and his stomach tumbled and he suddenly wanted to vomit. Kane and Braden repeated their well-timed act, sending the room swirling and rolling before Gates's swollen eyes. Kane picked him up again.

Martha Givins's screaming finally stopped them, brought a flashback of sanity over the room.

Braden grunted: "Take the damned fool to the saloon. He'll get more later when I get time. I'm a long way from bein' through with him. Now, move fast. Durand can't be far off, wherever he is. The bandages looked fresh."

They cleared the room, leaving the stunned Luke in Martha's arms. As they went out, he stirred and opened his eyes.

"They've gone," said Martha. "But they took Doc Gates."

"Oh, Lord. I'd better try to go down there."

"You'll stay right here!"

"Now, Martha, you know I can't let them do anything to Doc."

★ ★ ★ ★ ★

Doc Gates was conscious, but his legs refused to support him and he fell limply. Someone roughly retrieved him and threw him across a horse as if he were a blanket roll.

Braden mounted. "When you get him to the saloon," he ordered, "pour some red-eye down him. I want him in shape to talk fast and plenty. If he plays stubborn, Red Cloud'll have to hunt a new sawbones an' he'll never tend another man who's crossed me. Doc's responsible for pullin' Durand through. He must've slipped around at night like a coyote an' doctored him."

Cash Edmund pulled in beside his glowering boss. "We're losin' time here fast," he said with disapproval. "You can't dally on a hunt and catch the fox. Hear them shots a while ago? Sounded like all hell broke loose uptown. We missed the show by comin' down here."

Edmund's information irked Braden. "I didn't hear anything," he said irritably. "Why didn't you say something?"

"An' interrupt a man when he's enjoyin' himself? Not me. You was too tied up givin' the treatment to Doc. Red didn't hear the guns, either. I was on the porch and could hear 'em clear. They came real quick at first, then a few scattered shots."

With this new urgency pressing him, Braden did not pause for further details. Leaving horsemen behind to bring Doc Gates to the saloon, he swept away from the house with his horse at a run, Kane and Edmund hanging close by. Main Street's narrow strip showed empty at first, but, when they raced up to the Osage Girl, they found riders grouped.

A man rode out, calling: "Braden . . . Braden!"

"Hell, yes, over here," Braden answered. "What's up?"

"Two riders pulled out east from town."

"Why wait here? Get after 'em. Your orders. . . ."

"We tried that. One man got picked off, and every time we go down that way, some *hombres* cut down on us from the side streets. Can't get in close enough to spot 'em. I ain't that anxious to get salivated."

"You can't flush them, if you hang back," came Braden's retort. "Move in close when you can see the flash of their guns, then go after 'em. Might try usin' your head sometime. Now get off and split up. Red, you take a bunch and work down the south side of the street. Cash, you take the north side. Shoot anything that moves. They'll all be paid for. They can't stand up to us this way."

Kane and Edmund singled off their men and angled away sharply to opposite sides, not slowing until they reached protection of the building. Low-spoken orders were muttered and gunmen began stringing out.

So far not a shot had seen fired from the hidden marksmen down the now silent street.

Matt Braden sat his horse in front of the saloon like a field marshal watching his legions swing into line for action. Sight of these gunmen stalking through the night aroused in him a feeling of confidence, marking him with the awareness of his power. It wasn't that fear lay hidden within him, that their armed presence was required to lend him strength. He had never feared a man since his early border days, because he had always proved a match at barroom, rough-and-tumble fighting or with guns, and he had not been particular about the methods he employed. In the battle of the strong, he had been a giant in any joust.

Durand was the first man to instill a slight tinge of doubt as to his prowess in a showdown, but that was not fear; it was more like a keen antagonist who coolly weighs his chances and studies his man before making his bid. And this power uncoiling before him along the dull, danger-charged street, the only brand of power the border knew and recognized, acted on him as a sudden jolt of whiskey would on most men—warming and satisfying and strengthening. He waited for the battle to join, alert to the minute details of this fast-emerging scene—shadows bobbing here and there as men advanced, the wind steadily out of the south and its low, whistling play against the loose-jointed buildings. Matt Braden was enjoying himself for the second time this night.

Suddenly he thought his men weren't moving fast enough. At this stage, speed was paramount, so he rode along the north side to urge them on, to see what held them to their slow pace. There he stopped, eyes on the blurred figures. On the horse he presented a fair target, yet he did not dismount yet. He was unafraid.

A gun flamed down the street, a single red tongue licking out at him. A bullet sang past his head. A voice, clear and challenging, called out: "Stay where you are, Braden!"

Chapter Seventeen

The bold challenge surprised Matt Braden and quick caution forced him to dismount on the opposite side from which the shot had cracked, using the horse as a shield. The shouting voice nettled him, and, when he observed that his men had paused in their blurred stalking, he yelled out to them: "Keep moving!"

Whereupon the gun downstreet belched flame again with cold insistence and warning and Braden heard lead slam high up into the building behind him.

"Call off your pack, Braden!" the man behind the gun rapped back.

The wild plunging of his horse almost jerked Braden off his feet. The horse took precedence over the voice, now, and Braden cursed and iron-handed the frightened animal back. As the horse steadied somewhat, the thought bored into Braden with peculiar exhilaration that he and the man with the gun revolved in the core of this issue and that the street represented the dull, half-lit arena in which they would meet. Braden stepped backward, taking note of his open position, pulling the horse farther into the blank void edging the buildings. He expected the gun to flash again; however, it did not, and he shouted along to the men strung out on the north side: "Go after him!"

In decisive answer, the gun's harsh voice whipped back. Braden's horse was hit and plunging out of control with a surging wildness no man could hold down. He was forced to let the animal go or be dragged with it, and, as he gave up the reins, the entire street resounded to the rising roar of gunfire. Horses reared and broke from the tie racks and went racing away from the guns; shattered windowpanes crashed from wild shots, and lead made its ugly, singing whine everywhere.

At the spearhead of Braden's outfit on the north side, Cash Edmund crouched low against the wall of MacGregor's store. He had reached this post early and had not moved since the first shot. He had spotted the first gun's flashes on the same side, seemingly from the corner of a building, and saw them joined by others at short-spaced intervals along the lead-whipped street. After a close appraisal, he estimated from three to four men stood between him and Luke Givins's stable. Behind Edmund, men fired at the flashes, yet he merely held his gun in his right hand, not triggering a single shot, just waiting for this flame-tipped wrangle to crystallize into definite shape and trend. Where he pressed against the store front, the shadows cloaked thick and deep, like a depthless pool. Without much danger then, as he hadn't fired and revealed his location, he crawled to the building's end, holding his fire. And when a man rose wraith-like and booted feet raced a few paces along the boardwalk, he still did not fire. He wanted to work forward as far as he could without showing himself, for a plan had budded swiftly in his mind, evoking a queer sinister little smile that twisted his thin mouth into a hard, crooked line. It was as close as his solemn, hard features could broach a smile, and for him it revealed real pleasure, cunning as it was. Watching the flashes again, he counted positively this time—two men on each side. The moment was near for him to make his break. He possessed the patience of an Indian on a deer trail and his chance came as he expected: a Braden man showing himself on the far side and drawing fire.

As that happened, Edmund, a tight wiry form that blended with the shadows, ducked and sprinted noiselessly to his left, between MacGregor's store and the Lone Star café. And instantly, here between the walls, the thunder of the street battle became a muffled and distant racket as the wind tunneled through the narrow opening and he might have been standing between cañons instead of board walls. That queer, malignant smile touched his face again when he came to the end of the passageway, like an animal emerging warily from a rock den. He thought: *There'll be some surprises when I show up.* His unchecked maneuvering stirred new pleasure within him and he thought of other street fights and hill ambuscades for which he had always shown singular talent. Just a case of outsmarting the other man, he'd always told himself, and so far he had been dead right, With the heavy gun still in his right hand, he stepped to his right, assuming a peculiar, crouching stance, like a stalking animal, light-footed and nerveless and silent. Past the rear of three buildings he ranged, his gun swinging low and menacing. Another black, cramped opening appeared, and, flattening out against the wall, he peered into it. His eyes bored down its length. Satisfied, he advanced into the dark mouth. At the far end, a man hunkered down low, facing upstreet. Edmund edged closer; he must be sure. It was merely a case of being sharper than the other man. Halfway through he paused. He stood within certain range and the man apparently was oblivious to his deadly nearness. Now Cash Edmund leveled his gun and smiled. . . .

Jim Wyatt roved up the street from the stable, listening to the fading tattoo of hoofs traveling eastward. Subsequent relief was short lived as a horseman drove toward him, and down the street others were coming. The first horse broke into a ringing run, Wyatt slung his gun up and pulled once. The rider spurred faster and Wyatt pulled twice, in fast succession, at the blurred, fleeting form. Now the horse swerved away, riderless. From down the street, there was a slackening among the riders. While Wyatt reloaded, three men came running up to him.

"Durand got away," Wyatt told them. "But he needs a lead. It's all he can do to sit a hoss. Now split up . . . two on each side. Hold them a while, then fade out."

They were tall men, even for Texans, and Charlie Worth stood among them. Before they could break up, riders whirled at them from the west, forming a dark, moving mass that denoted power. Wyatt's gun *boomed* and the others joined in. A man gave a shrill cry, fell from his plunging horse under sharp hoofs, and suddenly riders were jerking back. Four guns, instead of one, faced them now. Wyatt's men split up, he and Worth posting themselves on the north side, waiting for another sally. It came presently as expected, but proved to be a half-hearted dash and the first shots beat it back. It was a waiting game now.

The last man shot from his horse groaned dully from the middle of the dusty street, and no one ventured to go to him. Wyatt was thinking: *We can pull out of here pretty soon.* But more horsemen rumbled up from the south part of town, joined the others down the street, and Wyatt knew a parley was taking place. Then it was that Wyatt heard a familiar voice urging his men ahead, saw a broad figure astride a horse, and called out his warning in hopes the showdown might be delayed to allow Durand more time.

That hope fell away on the rough roar of guns, heavier this time. Braden's gunmen pressed ahead until brisk fire forced them to halt and take cover. Wyatt and Worth switched posts several times, hoping to give the appearance of a stronger force. Accurate shooting was difficult in the dark, and thus far not a Wyatt man had been hit. You shot at a shadowy form or the flash of a gun. *Just a little while longer,* Wyatt thought, realizing that, once the fighting joined in close quarters, his men would be outgunned. That worry sent him running low back to Worth, who lay flat near the door of Lane's saddle shop as he sniped.

"Let's pull out in five minutes," said Wyatt.

"What's the hurry?" Charlie Worth's quick laugh was cut short by lead *whanging* into the wall beside them.

Wyatt did not wait for an answer and ran back. When a man on the far side rose and ran a few steps, Wyatt pumped two shots at him. There was no resulting cry and he knew that he had missed.

He steadied down, bent low, watching the shadows, and, when another man got up and ran jerkily, Wyatt's first shot sent him crashing from the boardwalk into the dust of the street. Movement ceased then, and gun flashes pinpointed the night as the fracas simmered down to a wild shooting match.

Wyatt, deciding the time was near to go for the horses at the stable, suddenly glanced across the street. Something had moved there, he thought. He froze low, eyes focused on the spot. Maybe he was seeing things, getting jumpy. Nothing moving there now, he decided, and swiveled his head to look around him once more before he eased back to where Charlie Worth lay. As he pivoted low, the figure of a man loomed between the buildings on his right, close and dangerous. Old, familiar warning signals flashed through Jim Wyatt; he fired instantly. Almost at the same time the man's gun flickered flame and lead smashed belatedly into the wooden wall near Wyatt's head. The Texan blasted three shots before he stopped. The slinking figure in the passageway was down, his gun silent. It was time to go. Wyatt wheeled. And from across the street, behind him in the dark pool where he thought something had moved, a gun blazed savagely. Wyatt was falling, his back and chest aflame. There was no light for him,

183

even upward, and a great, overpowering blanket of dullness was folding swiftly around him, and, so distant it might have been a hill echo, he heard a man shouting. . . .

Luke Givins, half running in his hurry, came to Main Street in time to hear the gun battle break into a full-throated roar. He worried about Wyatt and his friendly crew, but uppermost in his mind was Doc Gates, thin, drunken Doc, who wouldn't hurt anybody and was his own worst enemy. Fully aware of Matt Braden's frame of mind tonight, Givins knew that the little doctor likely was in for more rough treatment, possibly a terrible beating from which his slight body would never recover. Mingled with his liking for the doctor, and his admiration for his ability as a frontier practitioner, stirred a feeling of pity for a man who treated his body and great talents poorly. Why one blow from Red Kane's massive fist might kill the little doctor, he told himself fearfully. Deciding that Wyatt's cowpunchers could take care of themselves, he ran across the street to the stable. His face smarted and his shoulders ached from the pounding he had suffered from Braden.

At the next street north, he turned west, continuing until he found the alley that led to the rear door of the Osage Girl. Here he slowed up, picking his way with care and studying the narrow expanse. The *banging* of guns from the street alerted him to his old caution. The alley, dull and black and formless, was deserted to his eyes, not a single horse being tied behind the saloon, which was unusual. Up to the door he stalked, found it closed, and he stood there for a time, listening and breathing hard. The racket from the street blotted out any noise from inside, and he pressed the door open until he could peer inside through the narrow gap.

The rear of the place lay in darkness, but light from lamps

around the bar lit up the front. He had begun to doubt the hunch that had brought him here when, on the side opposite the bar, he saw Doc Gates tied to a chair, head hanging forward on his chest. Givins feared the worst for an instant. However, as he watched, Gates moved his head, his eyes on the batwing doors leading out into the street. Givins pushed the door open wider and gazed around the wide, low-ceilinged room. Where were Doc's guards? He saw no one and stepped inside, careful to close the door behind him. He had to be certain, so he crouched behind a poker table before crossing to Gates. The street's unbroken clamor fanned into the saloon in greater volume, filling the place with its roar and gunpowder smell. Just then a man pushed the saloon doors open and strode directly to Gates, who raised his head dazedly like a tired, defeated man only vaguely aware of his surroundings. The guard made a quick inspection and, satisfied that his prisoner was securely tied, swung a careless, hurried glance over the bar and clumped back outside to the gun play.

Luke Givins waited no longer. Running lightly, his boots made only a slight scuffing noise upon the sawdust-littered floor. With eyes shifting from Gates to the door, he whipped out a long pocket knife and slashed the ropes.

Gates looked up in surprise, his bloodshot eyes flickering with life and his dullness vanishing. As the last piece of rope lay snipped, he stood up and half ran for the back door at Givins's motion. Smart old Doc, Givins thought, he had them thinking he was finished. As the doctor went out the door first, Givins flung one last glance at the front. There was no sign of the guard and he hurried out. They turned north at the first street. After a short run they had to stop, for Gates was trembling and puffing.

Givins said: "There's a helluva gun battle goin' on back there."

Doc Gates waited until his heart slowed its hammering and his wind came back. "If that's Jim Wyatt," he said finally, "he'd better get out in a hurry. Guess it's him, because he's the only man in town with guts enough to face Braden . . . now that Durand's gone."

They faced south, unable to see the battle, but visualizing its action through sound and weighing the heavy odds against Wyatt. If the Texan had tarried too long? If he had jumped into a tangle from which he couldn't withdraw without exposing himself?

The guns died down for a short space, only to open up again in full cry. Givins muttered helplessly; he moved a few steps toward the firing. He felt old and useless. They were two old men standing in the dust of a darkened street in a hard-crusted cow town, witnesses to a savage clash involving friends, and there was nothing they could do about it.

Now, as they watched, a furious outbreak of shooting flared before them; it seemed to burst into flame on the north side of Main Street between two buildings, with a deadliness and finality unparalleled tonight; it seemed to arouse the entire street into action as other guns spoke out. Just as suddenly, the hammering of the guns shut off, like a great door closing out sound. There was a single shot here and there, until the town lay wrapped in thick, brooding silence.

Now what? Givins thought, his fear running full pace. He and Doc Gates, transfixed as they tried to weigh the full meaning of the action they could hear but see only in vague outline, next heard men running eastward toward the stable. Several shots crashed out and more men ran through the night. Soon afterward, horses traveled at a dead run and drummed away from the stable, racing southward from town.

The sound of those hard-running horses imparted new fear to the two men who stood silently reading fresh concern in the action. And hardly had the sound of the horses faded out when a big body of horsemen clattered eastward along the street, past the stable, and out onto the flat country.

To Luke Givins there was something inexorable and ruthless in the way that dark mass of riders swept out of town so rapidly after the other horsemen drove southward. Had Jim Wyatt held them off long enough for Durand and the girl to get away? He found himself wondering how far a wounded man could ride at a pounding, jolting gait.

He said thoughtfully: "Sounded like two horses goin' south, Doc. Wyatt had more men than that. Maybe all of 'em didn't make it. I don't like the looks of this." His thinking ran hard and blunt and he might have been talking to himself as he pondered: "That second bunch was Matt Braden, I guess." He knew the answer before he muttered it, although he wanted to think otherwise, to build up his ebbing hopes.

"Had to be Braden," said Doc Gates in a tired voice, fully as disconsolate as Givins. "Durand's in for it, if they catch him."

"He got a fair start," Givins said hopefully. "Doubt if Braden'll catch him tonight, but I dread to think of to-morrow."

There was nothing for them to do but move on, so, slowly, conscious of their helplessness, they began walking toward the stable and the dead calm of the street.

On second thought, Givins said: "We'd better steer clear of the street. Braden likely left a few men to watch the town, an' they'll be right sore about your getaway."

Doc Gates stopped suddenly. "I never thanked you for that, Luke. They planned to make me talk, but the shooting started too soon. Whatever they'd done to me wouldn't have been pleasant. Braden was simmering sore. I never saw a man with his hate. He'd enjoy seeing a wolf hamstring a calf, then hang around to watch the finish. So I'm thanking you now and again."

Both men fell silent and they came up to the stable full of dread at what might have happened up the street. Givins found himself wanting to go up the street to find out. He was fighting a sick feeling that refused to leave him and it all stemmed back to Wyatt and his cowboys. That sudden outburst of firing on the north side had a ring of finality to it. Now where were the other Wyatt men? He counted them over in his mind and remembered at least four, maybe five. Caution and common sense held him back, telling him it would be bad to go up to the saloons. He still had Doc Gates to think about. He'd go up after things quieted down. Another dead man tonight would not help.

Luke made up his mind immediately, and, with one searching look along the street, they crossed and started for his home.

Both men were dead tired, and, as they plodded along, their alertness deadened, they were not prepared for the tall man who stepped out from behind a shed and confronted them.

"Stop right there," he warned softly.

At first Luke feared it was a Braden man out snooping and watching, and then he cried out in recognition: "Charlie Worth! Put that damn' gun up!"

The three drew close together, hungry for the sound of a friendly voice.

Luke said: "We're goin' to the house, Charlie, come on. No time to talk here."

"No," said Charlie Worth. His voice was dull, bitter, lifeless. "Get me a hoss, Luke. I'm pullin' out."

Luke's glance switched about them in the shadows. The portent of Charlie's slack words, their dull, beaten tone, shook him, and the old prodding fear and dread that he had momentarily pushed down rose up and clutched him. *Better find out now,* he thought. So he asked quietly: "What is it, Charlie?"

It seemed a long time before Charlie Worth answered, and, when he did, the words came out brokenly and dryly and bitterly: "They got Jim Wyatt . . . shot in the back!"

Chapter Eighteen

Wind brushing off the prairie flung out its raw, clean smell and the stars hung brightly. But all this was lost on Walt Durand. Jim Wyatt's quiet warning to move out, the running horse, and the shooting—all told the story too well to his practiced ears. These happenings were retracing the well-traveled action ruts that always led to trouble. Durand's concern over Wyatt grew doubly real; it overshadowed any fear that Braden would race out of town after them, which he was certain to do eventually.

They rode without speaking, following a wide trail, until the flat lands on which the town squatted began humping up into the wide-sprawled foothills and scattered blots of timber. Durand soon discovered that the ride was helpful to him, reviving in part his old keenness and dulling the edge of his worry about Wyatt. He had paid no particular attention to the horse he rode, figuring it in his hurry to be one of Givins's trail-tempered geldings. But as Ellen, riding her regular saddle horse, continued to set a fast pace, he noted with sudden exhilaration the big-shouldered animal that carried him and discovered familiar lines and movement, especially that proud-flung neck and head. And with quick certainty he knew he rode the black stallion of Wyatt's remuda, the horse the Texan had presented him as a gift following the horse corral fight, the gift he didn't feel he should take because it meant a sacrifice. The black carried him like a feather and persisted in plunging ahead of Ellen's saddler. The stallion wanted to run. Again Durand felt the warmth of another debt he owed Jim Wyatt.

When the trail twisted back northward, Ellen pulled off and halted. "We go northeast from here," she said. "It's a long ride. How do you feel?"

"Good. I'm riding a rocking chair tonight . . . Jim Wyatt's stallion. He shouldn't have given me the best he had."

"He wanted to make sure you'd get there."

Durand made no answer and led Ellen farther off the shadowy trail into the timber. The horses' heaving made the only heavy sound among the thin-growing trees. Behind them, downtrail, no hoofs broke the murmur of the night insects. They listened a while and, with Ellen leading, rode back out and followed the trail. Ellen was a flying, elusive figure ahead of him, and the timber threw its shadowy veil across the dipping trail at intervals. The stallion had worn off his first testiness and settled down to eating up the distance, no longer trying to outrace the long-limbed saddler up front. Durand better understood Wyatt's reasons for picking the black. The stud was a natural road animal, covering the trail in great, unbroken, effortless strides with an amazing smoothness.

Twice Ellen reined up to inquire about Durand in an anxious, soft voice, and each time they drew off the trail to listen and wait and blow the horses. Near daylight, they got their first water at a still, shallow creek and clattered across its rocky ford. They were moving through broken range country, and, when the sun's first ruddy rays flashed out of the east, Ellen stopped again, as if looking for landmarks. Durand's drawn face caught her quick, penetrating gaze. Neither spoke. She found her markers and reined away slowly. Topping the crest of a hill, she looked down and pointed. A cabin's slate-gray hulk hunkered down below them; on the far side a rail corral sagged in its circular pattern. Farther on, a tree-flanked creek glistened dully under towering cottonwoods and wild elms.

"There it is," she said warmly, and rode downhill. She dismounted, with speed paramount in her mind, pushed the cabin door open, and went inside to look around. She came out and came quickly forward as Durand started to get off the sweat-flecked stallion. Her arms reached up to help him, and, as he swung down, his weight bumped heavily against her. She held to him, watching his gray face, not stepping back, half holding him to her. The full load of his weariness came to her now. He grinned thinly at his weakness and, staggering a little, made his way into the cabin as she supported his long, angular frame.

They found a crude two-bunk affair against one wall, and he sagged down upon the lower tier, eyes closed. For a long, endless moment she stood looking down at him, then inspected the one-room cabin with its mud-chinked walls and punctured roof where the light seeped in brokenly. She found a battered frying pan and coffee pot and meager supplies. This was a line rider's lonely cabin, used intermittently by men watching after the big herds that fattened on the waist-high creek bottom grass and rich uplands. From the looks of it, she decided it had not been used recently, a discovery that had its safety factor. A rough fireplace, well bedded with ashes from the last rider's visit, had been built at the rear. A blackened kettle hung at one side. She remembered the horses next, and, as she walked past the bunk, Durand lay sleeping, not moving from where he had first lain down. Going out to the horses, she led them to the creek and saw where a spring's clear stream fed into it. There was an urgency to her actions as she brought the horses back, unsaddled, and turned them into the corral.

While Durand slept, she started a fire and prepared a meal. A look at the supplies told her that, unless Wyatt brought food, they would be out in a couple of days. Afterward, she aroused Durand with reluctance, then watched him fade back into weariness and sleep after he had eaten.

He was still sleeping in early afternoon when she left to take the horses to water again. They showed an eagerness for the high grass in the lowland flanking the cabin, so she improvised hobbles from her saddle lariat. That sort of handling was not new to the gelding, but the stallion reared and fought, forcing her to compromise by making a rope halter and tying him to a corral post that still allowed him enough freedom for grass. The broad black back and rippling shoulders gleamed under the bright sun, and she watched in appreciation as he pulled strongly at the grass and raised the giant head and tossed the flowing mane.

A sound in the cabin pulled her back inside. She found Durand sitting up on his bunk, booted feet on the rough floor.

"There's no hurry to get up," she said. "Rest some more. Jim will be here tonight or tomorrow."

Mention of Jim Wyatt's name quickened his eyes and he ran a hand over his stubble-roughened face, presenting the picture of a taciturn man thinking hard, thinking back. He built a cigarette from the tobacco sack in his shirt pocket, sucked in the smoke with relish. But the pleasure went out of his smoke as he said quietly: "Jim's luck will have to be good. That smelled like an ugly gunfight to me. I saw one start like that in. . . ." He stopped short, displeased. He was talking about himself and he did not like that. His taciturn manner slipped back and he looked out the door to the dark creek line.

"Start where?" she asked softly.

"In Caldwell . . . and a dozen other places."

She saw that he had weathered the hard ride remarkably well, and now that he had rested, his restless, moving nature returned. He seemed to be preoccupied.

His thoughts kept shuttling back to Red Cloud and Jim Wyatt and Matt Braden. *What had happened back there in the street? Those shots?*

Not unkindly she said: "Walt, don't you ever get tired of fighting?"

He looked at her searchingly with faint surprise. "Yes, but once you start the ball rolling, you can't quit."

"You can pull out now," she reminded him.

"And let Braden take over?"

They were back on the same track that had resulted in the first breach between them.

"I don't mean for you to quit," she went on more warily. "But you push yourself too hard. You refuse to back up an inch. You can't go on like this always." And now a faint anger at him flared up and she exclaimed: "You're so bitter and hard . . . hard on yourself!"

He looked at her a bit sternly. "You've got to be hard with Braden's breed, Ellen. They shoot from the bushes if they can't get you any other way. That's why you have to be hard." He got up slowly and walked to the door, eyes on the creek. "And I don't want other men to do my fighting for me, to take my chances. I'm talking about Jim."

She stood up now and he faced her. Suddenly his face lightened, softening the hard line of his mouth. He smiled and he was a different man, and she thought: *I have changed him this much. I can do more . . . I can save him.* It was a rising gladness, a newly discovered power in her.

He towered above her, gaunt and tired, still hard and formidable. But a light burned in his eyes. He said: "I never used to worry about coming out of a scrap alive. I always knew I would. Now I'm going to worry."

"Why?" Her voice came low-pitched and tremulous. She was waiting for him and he came to her, his arms went around

194

her roughly and urgently, and her despair for him vanished as he kissed her. She did not pull back; her mouth, at first firm, yielded to a warm, compelling softness. They were alone and there was no strife-torn Red Cloud and its jumble of hates, no hard-bitten Braden, no swaggering Kane, no shadows, only a whirling rush of soft wind that curled about them. On his shoulders, Durand felt her arms, pressing and tight.

Finally he stepped back, arms still holding her. All the hardness and struggle had gone from his face now and she called to him as he had never heard a woman speak to him: "Walt. . . ."

And he still held her when the stallion's wild, rousing whicker rang out, and instantly he crossed to the gun belt that she had hung near the bunk. She saw him wheel back, gun in hand, his mind reaching out and beyond and away from them. When he went outside, his face had slipped back into its hard, watchful mask.

She did not follow him, but stood there slackly and a bit dully. One hand brushed her cheek. *A man kisses me,* she thought, *and I want to forget everything, even that they might ride in here and kill him.* She took a deep breath, feeling resigned, steadied herself, and stepped outside to look for Durand.

He was not in sight; the two horses grazed in the tall, wind-weaving grass. His absence evoked its cutting fear and she turned sweeping eyes over the rough hills and timber. There was a quick pounding inside her as Durand, walking with long, stretching strides toward her, came out of the brush behind the cabin.

His face showed no concern and she felt relieved. "I thought that was Jim coming," he said in a way that was also an apology for his sudden rush from the cabin.

"Or maybe Braden," she added.

Out here in the sunlight, his gauntness lay bluntly revealed; only his gray eyes blazed brightly. She read the weariness in his frame, that side of his body he favored, and she told him: "Go in the cabin and rest. If we have to leave tonight, you'll want to be stronger than you are now."

He smiled as if he must please her. They moved in front of the cabin. "I keep wondering about Jim," he said. "If things went all right in town, he could have ridden out here this morning or afternoon at the latest."

They decided to wait through the night for Wyatt before riding away. Durand thought critically if the peace of this cabin and the grass-rich lowlands and the slender young woman whose eyes rested on him had anything to do with his decision, and he knew they had. He liked this place; it would make a suitable homestead. Plenty of grass and water, although the cabin might be too close to the creek because of malaria, which was a plague almost in parts of the Territory. He reminded himself that he owed it to Wyatt to wait until the last moment. Otherwise, he and Ellen would leave the country. That thought had its cutting quality, for he knew he would have to come back to finish the job Larry Cramer has started and he had sworn to finish. His meandering, cloud-like reasoning, which was unusual for him, was leading him in a circle, he realized, for he always came back to Braden. He turned into the cabin and went to the bunk. He felt desperately worn in mind and body.

When Ellen touched him awake later, it was near sundown. The smell of food and coffee filled the cramped cabin. Standing beside the bunk, rather like a small girl, he thought, she said: "The horses are up and saddled. Nothing's happened. No sign of Jim."

He half nodded. He hadn't noticed it before, but her eyes seemed two shades of fathomless gray and blue. He got up stiffly, washed at the creek, and ate with a return of his trail-sharpened appetite. His side had a slight, itching feeling that was not unpleasant, and he knew that it was healing fast.

The sun died a glowing, sloping death in the west, coating the hills with the gray haze of dusk, then the darker hues of early night and, at last, the full mantle of darkness had been spread.

Durand sat smoking on the crude sill of the cabin door. He arose as Ellen came out and they walked over to the corral where the horses stood, still saddled.

"I don't like to leave a horse saddled a long time," he observed, "but it is best tonight."

They leaned against the corral rails. Durand's mind keep swinging inevitably to her, although whereas a boldness had urged him on that afternoon to hold her in his arms, a reserve and the pressing question of Jim Wyatt held him back.

"What if Jim doesn't come?" she asked.

"We'll have to go on. I'll take you to Elgin or some safe place."

He had only half answered her question and she said with impatience: "I'm not worried about myself. It's what you're going to do."

"I've made it all right this far," he countered evasively.

"I know that."

"If Jim fails to show up by morning, we'd better move on. Braden can't fail to find us forever."

She asked: "When you're completely well, are you coming back after Braden and Kane?"

"Yes."

There was no hesitation; he had spoken out evenly, like a man who had long since made up his mind.

She was silent, looking across the dim-lit bottomlands, burdened with brooding thoughts and a return of the old despair for him. She had known what his answer would be, although, somehow, she had hoped it would be otherwise, that there could be another way. She knew now there was none, and she reprimanded herself for thinking there might. She thought: *I've tried to make him turn back, and it is wrong. He'd have no pride, wouldn't be satisfied and content, if he did.*

He took her gently by the arm. "I'd like to take you and ride out of here to stay . . . if you'd go."

If she'd go! Softly her voice murmured back: "Why don't you ask me?"

"I will when I'm clear of all this."

"I hate to think of that. It'll be hard waiting and worrying about you."

"There's no other way out. The only reasoning Braden understands is behind a gun. He was made that way and he'll die that way, with his boots on. And remember, his bunch killed Larry. That's another reason why there's no other way."

"I know, I know . . . but. . . ."

He was holding her and her sweetness was slipping over him and the wind was curling back softly about them and he wanted to tell her in his rough, anxious way that he would take her with him now and forget all this; yet some inner rein held him back, checked him with a deep-rooted warning, and, in his whirling thoughts, he knew that he could not. And close against him, she kept remembering, like a low-tolled warning: *When I'm clear of all this.*

He held her for a long time, until the low-hanging, black shadows of the past were gone fleetingly. When, at last, they turned back to the cabin, the night was switching to a lighter overcast. He held her again, before she went inside, then he made a slow, searching circle of the cabin and angled up the trail to the rock-studded hill overlooking the cabin. The hills and timber stretched out in blurred, boundless masses from here. A whippoorwill uttered its distinct call and he ranged down the trail a way. He had not expected to hear any foreign noise. He wanted to walk and think this out, moved by the great pounding in his heart and his full-blown elation.

He stiffened with surprise when the sudden tattoo of a running horse cut across the night. He paused to make certain, listening, then moved to the hill's crest, where he stationed himself in the brush beside the trail, a few paces from where it snaked down to the cabin. At this point, coming up the grade, a tired horse would be traveling slowest. The hoof beat fell off, rapped out again, and faded away.

Somebody was running a horse when he could and walking or trotting it when he had to slow down. The horse drew nearer until Durand, beside the trail, heard hoofs against rocks at a steady clip and the bobbing outline of a single rider and horse shaped out. Closer, near the hill's top, the rider was framed as a bold silhouette against the sky. He seemed to be peering about and studying the trail and the hill and the timber. Durand stepped out onto the trail now, his gun covering the man. "Pull up!" he said sharply.

The rider sank his spurs into the tired horse's flanks, but Durand lunged forward at the sudden motion and grabbed the bridle, gun still swinging toward the saddle. As the horse reared, the rider sprang from the saddle against Durand, who clamped his good left arm around the man's neck and shoulders and muscled him to the ground flat on his back. Durand felt a little foolish when Luke Givins cried out lamely: "Walt, don't throw an old man around like this!"

They got up and Durand murmured a swift apology. "I wondered why you didn't pull a gun," he said.

"Where's Ellen?"

"In the cabin."

"Got here all right. No trouble?"

"Lucky, I guess. What's happened to Jim? Why didn't he come?"

"Let's go to the cabin. I don't want to have to tell this twice."

Chapter Nineteen

Luke Givins changed his mind before they had stepped half a dozen paces. Leading his fagged horse, he quietly told Durand about Jim Wyatt as they moved down the steep, rock-cluttered trail to the cabin. Durand stopped dead still at the news, and a windless, somber silence held the two men solidly, and Durand saw again, hauntingly, the tall, soft-voiced Texan urging him to ride off, then striding back into the cold, black core of the street where he was to die. *If Jim and his crew had come with us,* he thought bitterly, *we might have fought Braden off in the hills.* Yet he realized that Jim, with the keen appraisal of the seasoned gunfighter, had rightly reasoned that their little handful would be caught in the open and cut down mercilessly. First it was Larry Cramer to go, now Jim Wyatt. With a burning, helpless anger shaking him, he turned to Luke.

"Let's go to the cabin."

Durand rapped on the cabin door, quickly opened by Ellen.

He said tonelessly: "Luke got in." Then he told her about Jim Wyatt.

She stepped back with a sudden exclamation, and Durand went in and lit the lantern on the table.

In the corn-yellow light, Luke Givins showed the strain of his hard ride in his brush-torn flannel shirt and Levi's, in his sunken, red-rimmed eyes, and old, sagging shoulders. He gulped a cup of cold coffee and stood looking at Durand, thinking: *What will he do now?* He hated to tell the rest of the story, because all of it was bad.

Durand said: "Tell us, Luke."

Luke finished his coffee first. In a dull voice, he began:

Fred Grove

"Braden is our worry now. His men are swarmin' the hills everywhere." He punctuated his warning with a sweeping wave of his hand. "They're after you, Walt, with orders to shoot on sight. That's what they're saying in the saloons. I slipped out of town as soon as I could. Saw bunches of riders three times. They don't know this country like me. I rode around 'em and through 'em."

Luke, still eying Durand, waited for the tall man to speak. But nothing was said, and Luke, trying to keep his recital matter of fact, continued: "All I know about the fight is what Charlie Worth told me an' what I picked up here an' there. Jim an' three of his boys went down the street that night to hold 'em off a while, as you know. Charlie says the plan was to tie Braden up for ten or fifteen minutes. Then everybody was to fall back an' grab a hoss at the barn. It worked slick as a greased wagon wheel at first. Them Texas boys can sure throw the lead in the right places, an' mighty fast. They knocked Braden's gun slingers back every time they came in close. Now Jim was right ahead of Charlie on the north side of the street. It came time to run for the hosses. Just then a man tries to bushwhack Jim from the north side. Guess Jim dusted him dead center an' mighty quick because the other gun stopped when Jim was still standin' up there, big an' strong an' grand. Like a wild stallion trapped in a box cañon, Charlie said."

Luke paused and Ellen filled his coffee cup again. Luke's glance switched again to the tall man. *Would he go down like Jim Wyatt, gun smoking and stubbornly refusing to back up a step?* Luke guessed he would.

"Charlie scrambled up to help Jim if he could," Luke related. "But it was too late. Charlie raved like a wild man when he told it. A gun cracked out from the other side. Charlie says it was Red Kane an' he was roarin' something. The one part

202

Charlie remembers was Red shoutin' to Jim . . . 'Damn you . . . I'll give you what I gave that marshal in the hills.' Jim's gun stopped and the other Texas boys had to get the hell outta there. Me an' Doc found Charlie a little while later on the south side of main street. I gave him a hoss to get away on, but he swore he'd come back. Braden an' his crew batted outta town after you, right after they got Jim. The next mornin' Doc an' me buried Jim out there with your partner . . . Reverend Anderson an' your father was there, Ellen. . . . Before we laid him away, Doc looked him over. Kane had drilled him in the back . . . five times! Died right there in the street, with his gun in his hand." Luke swallowed hard, then added: "Jim wasn't the only man that died with his boots on. That was Cash Edmund tryin' to get Jim from the north side. He had more holes in him than a spliced bridle. Jim could sure handle a gun. Mighty near as fast as you, Walt."

Walt Durand stood like a tall pine beside the table, his dark head slightly lowered, his hands hanging loosely. But his eyes—they held a peculiar fascination for Luke Givins. They narrowed and seemed to see everything, yet saw nothing; they were cold and gray and hard like flint. Luke looked uncomfortably at Ellen. She, too, watched Durand, aware of a terrible resignation.

What would he do now? She feared he would ride straight back for Red Cloud. She said: "Walt." He didn't answer and she repeated his name.

He looked up then. There was no passionate outburst as Givins had expected, just the all-powerful, grinding hardness glaring from his eyes. He was cold as a hammer as he said: "Better get some sleep before we ride."

"I know a rancher at the edge of the hills," Luke said. "Get there an' we're safe."

Durand left them and walked from the cabin to the corral.

The stallion snorted at his approach and wheeled powerfully away to the far side. Watching the blurred shape of the big horse, Durand thought grimly: *So it was Red Kane, after all. Not Crawford, who died with a snarl on his face in the cañon. But Crawford was with Kane when they ambushed Larry. The hoof prints showed that. I thought it was Smoke's work . . . it was his style . . . from the bushes and in the back. That's one reason why I waited for him in the cañon. I'm glad I got him. Now Kane gets Jim in the back. It's the style up here.*

Durand moved away and climbed the hill, thinking heavily. Here his weariness and the partially healed wound hit him. In the center of the rough trail he stopped, head sagging and shoulders bent a little from their usual erectness. And, for the first time, like a coyote sneaking out of the timber, came the thought that he could ride away from here with Ellen to a new land for a new start and let Matt Braden have his Red Cloud and rule the range with an iron, brutal hand, let Red Kane continue his swaggering dominance and ambush any man fool enough to interfere with him. It was a new temptation to him, tantalizing for the moment, made more attractive by his weariness. Hadn't he met Braden and Kane at every turn with ready guns? Hadn't he waited out that slick, fast-hand gunman, Smoke Crawford, and with Charlie Worth recovered the stolen remuda? He had done all these things, he told himself.

Now suddenly, from below, the stallion whickered boldly. It was like a bugle call in the stillness, tingling and commanding, and Walt Durand raised his head up straight, listening. There was an awe in the stallion's call, something that filtered through him with singular directness and compulsion. Once before, in Braden's hang-out in the hidden valley, he had heard the stallion's blast and he had answered it. Then it had come when he was undecided, at the point of turning back; it had rung out again, like a trumpeting omen, when he was wavering. It was quiet again now, the heavy stillness creeping back like a rising stream.

Durand straightened, remembering many things, and walked back down to the cabin, a sudden loathing for his weakness rising in him. Inside, he lay down on the floor beside Luke and slept, the stallion's whicker still lance-sharp in his mind.

Two hours before daybreak, Durand aroused Luke, then Ellen, who slept on the bunk.

As Ellen cooked breakfast, Luke said: "This rancher's place is on the east rim of the hills. I figure it's better'n a day's ride from here."

"We can make it," Durand said. The idea was to reach some place where he could leave Ellen, rest up, and come back to see this issue through to the bitter end. He would have to be right when he returned, rested and sharp. No misses.

With a pallor lighting the sky in the east, Luke led away and they splashed across the rock-bottomed creek. By daylight, they were pushing steadily through thick patches of timber blotting the bulging hills. Luke rode in front, with Ellen in the center. There was no trail to follow, which slowed them. They made their first halt with the sun well up.

Durand, darkly silent and grim, caught the quick attention of Luke, who said: "You look tuckered, Walt. I'll go back to that last high hill and look over the back country while you rest."

As Luke drummed away, Durand dismounted; his weakness sent him sagging against the stallion, who danced away. His boots were leaden weights, and in his eyes objects took on a peculiar proportion. He realized, warningly, that the strength built up resting at Red Cloud had been rapidly expended during the first long night ride. While Ellen tied the horses, he propped his back against a jack oak and looked back the way Luke had vanished, and Ellen recognized the same unchanging, flint-edged look she had glimpsed in the cabin when Luke recited his story. Durand had scarcely spoken since then, although she knew his eyes had followed her often.

"Stretch out and rest," she suggested.

"This tree is soft enough. I want to see what's behind us. You know," he added wearily, "this gives me a chance to feel like a man on the dodge. I've always been on the other end until lately, chasing the other fellow. Now the pack's after me." His gaze still clung to the back stretches, and suddenly he said: "I wish you were out of this, Ellen. I'd like to put you on that black stallion, head him east, and quirt him hard."

She sat down beside him. "You'll have to tie me on if you try it. Nothing would happen to me if Braden did catch us. You're the one who needs to be away from here . . . as far as you can get."

"I don't want to go too far. That would make it harder to get back."

"It would be better if you didn't come back."

"No."

"Walt," she said earnestly, her gray eyes serious, "I don't want you to take chances on my account. I'm not afraid."

A thin smile flickered across his taut face, and its slack dullness sent a rapid jolt of fear through her. "Braden is not a gentleman," he said dryly, "though he may look like one. He wouldn't let a woman stand in his way to get a man. Not even a woman like you. Remember that if anything happens."

While they waited, Durand dozed. Sleep seemed to come to him as soon as he tilted his head back and stopped talking.

He looked taller and more gaunt than she had ever seen him and she noticed his flushed face, beaded by fine sweat, and swiftly she feared that the fever had returned. Her hand, when she touched his forehead, came away wet with sweat. He stirred and she got up and took the canteen tied to her saddle horn. He raised up on his elbows, took a long pull, and lay back, stretching out fully this time in the sparse shade. A late morning drowsiness, pitched to the low drone of insects, came on listlessly and the heat bore down in the windless timber.

Presently she turned from him to look back over the country into which Luke had ridden. Before her stretched a narrow strip of prairie backgrounded by rolling, tree-studded hills. She could see the top of the hill that Luke planned as a look-out, but, from here, the timber hid any movement. What was keeping him? It was close to an hour since he had left. He said he would scout the surrounding country from the high vantage point, and he had had more than enough time to do that, she figured.

Suddenly Durand sat up. "Luke back?"

She did not answer, her attention held by the muffled beat of a running horse approaching from the west. It sent a shiver of excitement through her. Luke, a great lover of horseflesh, wouldn't be moving like that on a blazing day unless it was an emergency.

They both stood up and Durand said softly: "It'd better be Luke." He held a black gun in one hand.

The hoofs came on at a hard, tingling tattoo, and then from out of the timbered thickness rode Luke, low in the saddle like an Indian jockey. In the open, he straightened up and raced the sweat-streaked animal over to them, excitement glittering in his old eyes.

"Riders west o' here," Luke panted.

"Braden?" Durand asked.

Luke nodded assent. "Couldn't pick out the men, but the hosses looked familiar an' I saw the sun flashin' on their rifles. That was enough for me."

"How many?"

"Five . . . maybe more. They rode out fast into a little opening where the timber peters out and stopped. One man got off and went over the ground like he was huntin' Spanish gold. When he waved the crew over for a look-see, I took the hint and lit out. I reckon we'd best git fast, Walt."

"Let them come," said Durand. His eyes took in the girl and Luke at once. "I've been thinking we'd better split up. Luke, you. . . ."

As they stared at him, surprised, Durand was thinking: *I'll only hold them back in a long race. Yet I haven't told her.* . . . His thinking had suddenly become fuzzy and he felt wooden and ineffectual. Time was an overwhelming, crushing factor. He wanted to stop and fight. He wanted to ride the stud ahead alone, to draw Braden after him. He wanted Luke to take Ellen out of here where it was safe. He wanted. . . .

Luke said frantically: "For gawd's sake, Walt, make up your mind! Ellen, git the hosses!"

Wide-eyed, she ran forward and in her abruptness caused the stallion to plunge and pull on the tied reins. Ellen stopped. If the stallion broke away now. . . . Durand turned around. Luke cursed helplessly under his breath. But the reins held for the moment, and Durand edged in, unknotted them, went up to the powerful black, and mounted so quickly the wound made him wince. Ellen was up now. She fastened piercing, accusing eyes on him. "We're all riding together," she said decisively, and he noticed the hurt expression as she spoke.

Luke whirled his horse, looking strangely at Durand, still

puzzled by the lack of decision he had shown. Hell, Durand must be worse off than he'd figured. As they raced eastward, Luke threw a quick look behind them. The woods revealed nothing, but he knew riders moved back there somewhere, and he remembered sun flashes on rifles. . . .

Red Kane, leading a bunch of riders made surly by the lack of breakfast and fruitless searching, discovered the line cabin early in the morning as they topped the rise and looked toward the creek. With him rode the Cherokee, an acquisition to the crew since Smoke Crawford was killed, and four nondescript hands who fitted the pattern of men along the Territory border who lived by their guns and fast horses. The Cherokee, a thick-chested man with prominent cheek bones and piercing black eyes, had taken on added stature since Crawford's demise, although he had not participated in the Red Cloud gun battle with Jim Wyatt's Texans. At that time, he was ramroding a bunch of stolen horses through from central Texas, across Red River, past Territory marshals and into Kansas, where you could always peddle a fine horse, no questions asked. Now, with Cash Edmund buried, the Cherokee filled the requirements of a hard-boiled, alert lieutenant who took particular pleasure in following orders to the finest shade. That the Indian, who claimed to be a fullblood but was whispered to be half Mex, was hard and liked the going rough was soon evident to Braden, a keen judge of men, who immediately sent him a summons to the headquarters hang-out right after the Red Cloud showdown. The Indian caught them triumphantly as he rode an exhausted horse into their makeshift creek camp while they rested from hunting for Durand.

"You're hell on a horse," Red Kane greeted him critically. He did not like the Indian, but they needed him.

"Worse on men," the Cherokee reminded him. "The boss said he wanted this Durand man dead. I feel sorry for him already."

The Cherokee's grim humor was lost on Kane, who said: "Your job is to do some fancy trail work. Braden says you're a good tracker. We're trailin' two horses. Lost their trail over a rocky ridge. It petered out all at once."

In his mocking, superior way, the Indian said: "The trail is there . . . if you can see it."

"That's your job . . . to find it," Kane snapped, and walked away.

The Cherokee's eyes were good. Retracing the point where the tracks had faded out, he dismounted, grunted to himself, and went over the rocky footing like a bloodhound. He shook his head once and grunted again.

At last he looked up significantly at Kane, smiled with self-satisfaction, got back on his horse, and reined off through a cluster of close-growing timber instead of following the open and easier route. A short distance in, he leaned over and pointed down where the ground lay scuffed. "Here it is, white man," he said, smirking at Kane.

"Ride ahead and follow it fast," the foreman rapped back at him violently. "We ain't on a horse-stealin' night act . . . we're manhuntin'!"

The Indian's poker features tightened for an instant. He had no respect for the white men with whom he thieved. Then he plunged spurs deep into his horse and spurted ahead, eyes on the ground, as he followed the faint trail at a fairly rapid pace.

So it was the Cherokee who led them up to the cabin the next morning. Word had been sent north to Braden, working with another group, when the trail was picked up again, and now Kane ordered a welcome rest at the cabin while they waited for the boss to catch them.

Braden, riding a heavy-set red roan, caught them sooner than expected. He came charging down the steep incline to the cabin with six men behind him and, after Kane tolled off the news, insisted on going through the cabin first. He saw where the crude bunk had been slept in, and noted fresh ashes in the stove.

"These ashes feel warm," Braden told Kane, and went on looking. He thought he was right, but he wanted to make certain about the rider with Durand.

"What're you lookin' for?" asked the puzzled foreman.

Braden turned back to the center of the cabin, eyes roving the small room like a circling hawk. His next move was panther-like. He lunged to the rough table, bent under it, and came up with something. Ignoring Kane, he looked at it with eager, searching eyes. It was a light blue scarf, with a faint, pleasant scent, a woman's scarf. He had seen it before when he rode with Ellen Winston. So she went with him, ran off, you might say. Durand was getting the woman, too. Braden clutched the scarf like an Indian waving a scalp. His old hunger for her came back with a burning rush, and he knew now it had never left him, never would; it also returned his punctured pride, blasted hopes, and depthless hatred for a single man. Only through Durand could he reach her now, and this he would do.

Matt Braden wadded the scarf into a tight ball, hurled it to the floor, and, eyes like hot coals, tramped past Kane outside where men and horses waited. When they crossed the creek, it was Matt Braden who plunged out in front, Matt Braden who set a horse-killing pace, Matt Braden who lashed out with biting words when a rider lagged. . . .

Luke and Ellen knew how to get the most out of a horse,

and what Durand lacked today, the black made up. The race soon developed into a wild, punishing test for Durand, and the country blurred into a jumble of broken country, which was gradually giving way to wide, sloping stretches of prairie. Once, when Durand glanced back as they rode up an incline, he thought he saw movement far behind them. He said nothing but was certain the dark blot meant horsemen cutting across open prairie. When he looked a second time, however, the moving mass had disappeared in the vastness.

Now a new menace faced them. The rapid going, coupled with the searing heat of the prairies, was taking its certain toll of the horses. If they rode on tonight, which they must do if they were to reach the rancher's place, they would be forced to rest the horses. Even the big black was beginning to show the strain, and Luke's animal, a steady saddler, stumbled now on rough ground. Ellen's horse, carrying the lightest burden, was holding up stronger. Shortly, when a narrow valley cutting east-west unfolded between shouldered hills and they found a tree-shadowed spring, they halted, watered the horses, and sat huddled under the trees, all eyes bent westward. Dusk would creep in soon.

Durand, sober-faded and weary, looked to his guns. Often Ellen felt his eyes upon her, but there was nothing soft about him now. He seemed to be weighing their chances in his hard way. They were tired and they talked little.

Luke, watching the horses, said quietly: "They're anxious, like us, to know when this'll be over. If they carry us five more hours, we'll beat Braden."

Dusk clamped down and wrapped the spring pool in thick purple.

Durand got stiffly to his feet. "Are they ready to go, Luke?"

"Reckon so. Have to be, don't they?"

After that they struck out east up the valley. Sounds take on an added distinctness at this hour before the earth casts off its light mask of dusk and plunges into darkness, and when a horse whickered up ahead of them, it broke the stillness, clear and ringing.

Durand, in the lead, felt a tightening deep inside him. He halted, and Ellen and Luke looked at him fearfully. Had they waited too long at the spring resting the horses?

"We'll have a look," said Durand coldly. He kicked his horse into a trot. Here the valley made a slight bend, and, when they rounded it, he checked his horse and waved them back. There at the mouth of the valley, framed darkly, two riders were etched in bold outline.

As Durand pivoted the stallion, Ellen and Luke near now, a rifle snarled behind them, its leaden blast hissing overhead.

Chapter Twenty

The Cherokee was a killer of horses, like Red Kane said, but he also could cover ground with the swiftness of a raiding war party. So when Matt Braden sighted horses through the shimmering heat waves, he quickly yelled the stone-faced Indian over.

Eyes dancing with triumph, Braden said decisively: "We got them now. Take five men with the best horses and cut them off. We'll follow and close in. Ride the horses into the ground if you have to. But get in front of Durand, head him off."

The Cherokee smiled and rode off at a gallop with riders singled out by Kane. They began an angling ride slanted to move in ahead of their quarry.

Braden whipped the other men together and told Kane: "Ramble or that Indian will beat us to our pleasure."

Kane looked sullenly after the Cherokee, who was at that moment rushing out of sight through broken timberland. "He'll make it if he don't wear out his spurs and quirt," he said.

Long shadows were beginning to coat the draws and low places when Braden, pushing a dead-weary horse, spied the slash of a valley ahead. He stopped and the roan stood beaten, head down. Kane came up and other riders straggled around them. Braden sat silently, eyes on the day's last light playing atop the hills overshadowing the valley. He felt growing misgivings about his plan. It was a pure gamble, although a good one taken in the face of necessity. He had not seen the fleeing horsemen since he had hurried the Indian off on the horse-killing dash. Who was the third rider? It made

no difference; they were all running and were outnumbered.
But what had happened to them and where was that damned
wild Indian? There was nothing to do but go on and find out,
he decided.

They rode warily up to the valley's entrance, scanning it
closely, for its wooded roughness offered ambush possibilities. Late twilight bathed the valley floor with its thickening
mantle. A night bird voiced its first tentative call; the roan's
hoofs striking the limestone rang out hollowly. Then, up the
valley, the *clatter* of trotting horses broke out. Braden pulled
up. The movements, at first sharp in the stillness, padded
away eastward like dying drumbeats. Hard upon these
sounds came the *boom* of a single rifle through the early darkness, which was like a tonic to Braden.

"The Cherokee made it!" he cried to Kane. "Come on!"
And he flung his horse toward the sound of the gun. . . .

Twisting low in the saddle, Durand got in one shot, then
the bend was before him and he swept around it on the run,
feeling the stallion's shoulder muscles bunch under him as he
lunged out in quickening stride. Ahead of him, surprisingly,
Luke and Ellen had halted and he wondered why. He started
to yell them on, but Luke shouted warningly: "Hosses comin'
from the other end!"

And downvalley now, darting shadows pounded toward
them, and the blunt fact hit home to Durand that they were
blocked from either end of the valley. Durand opened up on
the onrushing horsemen and Luke followed suit with a six-
shooter. A horse shook the ground as it went down, followed
by a rider's violent yell. Suddenly the rush had been checked;
the dark line of men and horses melted back into the long
shadows. From the other end of the valley there was no movement, and Durand, thinking of rock and timber cover, called

Fred Grove

out to Luke and Ellen to ride that way.

They rode at a gallop to the north side, and, when they turned to look back, Durand said coldly: "They'll have to cross that opening first. Give me your rifle, Luke."

Luke jerked the rifle from its saddle holster and handed it over, but he couldn't take his eyes off the area where the horsemen had pulled back. They got off and led the horses farther into the timber. Then they came back and waited. The valley lay wrapped in disarming silence. From here a horseman moving toward them would be dully marked against the night.

With the rifle resting across his arm, Durand said softly: "We'll have to make a break for it, but not now."

"Where?" Luke asked. "This hill behind us is almost straight up. A horse can't climb it."

"I'll look around and see."

Luke, thinking hard over their chances, did not answer. Ellen slipped back to them after another look at the horses, and they talked in low tones. They expected to hear horses out in front of them, but none came, and the night noises settled down to a steady murmur.

Durand made Ellen get behind a tree for protection, and, as they stood close, he felt her hand touch his arm lightly. His arm went around her quickly, and he saw the shadowy outline of her face turned up to him. He held her, then let her go.

Her voice came almost a whisper: "Where are you going?"

"To look around. I'll be back."

His tall figure blended with the night and she was left there thinking of the gentleness of this tall man, and, although she could not see his face, she remembered the shape of his mouth when he smiled slowly, the deep, gray, searching eyes, and the hardness that had gone out of them at the cabin when he held her. Still thinking of him, she left the tree and found

Luke looking off across the blackened valley.

He turned nervously. "Better get back there. It's safer."

"I'll stay here with you."

He did not argue the finality in her answer. He was thinking of Martha and that they had come so close to getting away. If they hadn't paused to rest the horses. . . . But his reasoning told him the horses couldn't have continued far without playing out. This way there was a chance. Maybe they should have split up as Durand suggested. *No, that was bad planning, too. There was a chance,* he told himself doggedly, *a slim one. And Durand, though near exhaustion, was more like his old self again, taking the lead and thinking, instead of hesitating as he had that afternoon. That hesitancy,* he decided, *could be traced to Ellen.*

While Luke watched, a tiny point of flame appeared down the valley; it leaped higher and higher, boldly and mockingly. Ellen had seen it, too.

"Pretty brave, ain't they?" Luke observed. "They know they got us cut off. That's like Braden to rub it in, makin' a campfire so we can see it. He ain't forgot he was sweet on you, an' I reckon he'd get his whole crew killed to be sure of Walt." Ellen moved and Luke put in hastily: "Now I don't mean it's your fault. Lord, no. It just happened they both went after the same girl. If I was a young feller, your dad would have to chase me off every night with a shotgun."

"I wish you were home with Martha," said Ellen feelingly.

"Well, I ain't . . . an' I wouldn't run off if I could. Martha wouldn't want me to."

Ellen patted his thin, bony shoulder. "I know you wouldn't, Luke."

The night seemed timeless, dragging on unchanged, which stirred in her a brooding fear for Durand and revived old memories: the earnest and direct way he talked, the almost boy-like shyness and hunger he showed at mention of certain things, a home, for instance, perhaps a woman. She bit her lip to keep it from trembling, and looked out another countless time into the darkness. Would he come back to her? Was he marked for the same end as Larry and Jim? They had been resolute men, too, capable of taking care of themselves.

Footsteps broke the silence. Luke stiffened and moved his gun. A low call came out of the darkness.

"Luke. . . ."

"Sure, Walt," answered Luke.

Now Durand crossed over to them.

"See that fire?" asked Luke. "Pretty sure of themselves, ain't they?"

"We're well covered here," said Durand, and Ellen seemed to feel his eyes touching her. "When they built that fire, I was up close. Most of their men are over there. They must figure we'll try that end. Well, it's going to be the other way. If we don't move, we'll be pickings in daylight. Now a man can lead a horse till he gets to the bend where we turned back. That means something."

Luke thought it over. "A rough chance, but a chance. We can't stay here. I have no hankerin' to be buzzard meat."

There was a short silence, and Durand broke it with: "Luke, come back to the horses with me. The black's got a stiff shoulder."

"Sure," said Luke, catching something urgent in Durand's tone.

They left Ellen on watch and walked back to the horses. Once Ellen thought she heard Luke's voice rasp out sharply in argument, but that was all. When they returned, it was decided they would make the break shortly before daylight.

Luke suggested: "We'll need some sleep. Take the first watch, Walt."

Lying wrapped in Durand's long slicker, back in the timber where she could hear the horses stamping, Ellen thought of Durand. And a chill gripped her. When he came back from the horses, he had spoken to her only briefly and given her the slicker. Her uneasiness grew colder, something apart from the dread of the run through the valley's end, but it was too vague and elusive for her to grasp and she fell asleep with it unraveled.

Touching her arm, Luke awakened her. She looked at the sky. Something stirred her. She said: "But it's getting light. Walt said we'd leave before daylight."

"We're leaving later," said Luke.

His answer wasn't satisfactory to her. He might have been soothing a little girl.

Ellen threw back the slicker, got up, and glanced quickly at the saddled horses. Her head tilted up, fixed in attention. Only two horses stood there. The great-bodied black of Durand's was gone! She turned and came back to Luke, almost stumbling.

"He's gone! Luke, tell me!"

Stung by her accusing tone, Luke put an arm around her. "Yes, he's gone, Ellen . . . you see."

She whirled away from him and started for the horses.

He caught her. "I'll tell you," he said helplessly. "An' God forgive me. He told me last night. There wasn't anything wrong with the black. He decided not to take a chance of you gettin' hit, which was almost certain. We're waitin' right now for that bunch at the west end to ride past us when they hear the guns. That'll leave one end of the valley open, like Walt figured. We'll bust out of here . . . back to Red Cloud. I promised him I'd take you back. . . ."

Something had gone out of her; she was all emptiness,

drawn and dead. Dully she asked: "Was that all he said? No word for me . . . ?"

"No," Luke began, "he said he'd come back for you. . . ."

Luke faltered futilely, and she finished it for him: "After he gets Matt and Red."

Luke turned away, hating to face her. "That's exactly what he said, Ellen."

She made no answer. Light was breaking swiftly across the sky. They stood woodenly, Luke straining for sounds from the valley. Then it came—gunfire beating out furiously from the east. It was like a death knell to her, and all she could see was a tall man with a slow smile and the light touching his hard eyes. . . .

Durand stood his watch and took his brief snatch of sleep. He rose at once when Luke stirred him. "Time to go," said Luke. Durand went slowly to the horses, feeling the drag of early morning sluggishness. He had slept but little. When the stallion stood ready, he led him to the edge of the timber. Here he hesitated, gave the reins to Luke, and walked back. He looked down at her, and all the aches of memory came over him in one bitter rush. *If I get back,* he thought, *if I get back.* . . .

Luke was waiting for him. They shook hands. Neither spoke; there was nothing to be said. They separated now, an old man, bent with hard riding, watching with burning eyes a lean man leading a horse off into the darkness up the valley.

Durand looked downvalley. The campfire was out. A faint flush smeared the sky in the east. He traveled deliberately, the stallion padding behind him. They came to the bend. Durand took one last look back where Luke and Ellen were and swung up into the saddle. *Time to go again,* he thought, and prodded the horse gently, turning now, until the dark maw of the timber-choked valley loomed ahead. . . .

The Cherokee stood guard near the faint trail that wound through the valley. He flung another contemptuous glance westward and saw nothing. *Braden is too cautious*, he thought. *Both ends are plugged tighter than a whiskey barrel, and those people in between know it.* He was hungry and fagged and this continual watching irked him while the four men behind him slept snugly in their blankets. No smoking, Braden had said after the Indian sent a rider around to contact the main body of riders. *To hell with that*, he thought. He rolled one then, swiftly, and lighted it, cupping the match in his hands. It was this momentary flare of light that Durand saw as he closed in. The Indian, sucking in the smoke hungrily, heard the muffled passage of the horse. He flung the cigarette away and reached for his gun, but, before the whirling finger of fire had touched the ground, flame leaped from the gun of the man on the horse, and the Indian went down without firing a shot.

Durand jumped the black through the trees and the horse crashed ponderously against saplings, righted himself, and moved ahead with a lunge as men shouted and ran from their blankets. Durand felt his first real hope of this fading night stir him as the horse broke clear and light filtered ahead through the timber. But now a man stood directly on the trail, his gun aflame.

Durand rode the black over him and heard hoofs strike soddenly on flesh and the man scream. They were free for the instant, and, on the heel of this elation, he thought back to Luke and Ellen. It was time for Braden to come fanning out from the other end, for Luke and Ellen to ride in the opposite direction. He was already thinking and planning ahead when, as he pounded around a sloping, rock-layered hill, the black faltered in his long stride as if held from behind. Durand dug in with his spurs. The animal responded strongly at first, but was soon slowing, now blundering, now staggering. The gunman they had ridden down on the trail, Durand thought grimly, and slipped from the saddle. Making one last effort to keep his feet, the stallion went down with a *crash*. Durand stepped over and looked down at the horse, shook his head, and ran to a growth of jack oaks, hunkering down low to wait this out to its bitter, certain finish. Carefully he reloaded the one gun he had used. It was fully light now, early in the day for a man to die. Every noise in these hills was clear and near to him. And he looked up at the sky, all clean and fresh.

He knew they would come tearing along the trail soon enough. In fact, they came sooner than he expected, although he was as ready as he could ever be. In the early sunlight, he picked out Matt Braden leading his men around the hill, with Red Kane riding at his left stirrup. The others didn't matter, just those two. *Even this,* he thought, *is better than a dusty street of a cow town or a deathbed.*

Braden had found the downed horse. He couldn't miss that magnificent body, slanting across the trail, his great head pointing forward where the last beat from his heart had driven him before he bled to death. The crew looked at the horse; Durand, crouching in the jack oaks, heard them mutter. Now was he to be denied Braden and Kane? The big man had waved riders ahead of him. They came on, but slower, eyes on the trees. They knew he couldn't be far off. They spotted him, and the sun glittered on an upraised carbine. Durand fired first; the man fell from his horse, lay there as if stunned, then began crawling back.

It was a cavalry charge now, the kind his father used to tell him about up north on the plains. Only these men were not Sioux. Lead *whanged* through the trees, picked out chunks of bark, sent them flying. He knocked down a horse and scrambled back a bit. He turned again and snapped a shot at Braden as he ran from his horse. Kane, afoot, too, came up with Braden. Durand waited. *Let them get closer,* he told himself.

The timber was quiet for a very short time and he suddenly heard firing down around the hill. Now Braden moved to another tree. Durand shot, missed. Kane was coming up on his right, slipping through where the timber was thickest. *One at a time,* Durand thought, and he lunged to his right behind a tree. He stepped out and Kane faced across at him with boring eyes. And in that instant before he pulled the trigger, Durand knew he would always remember the crouching figure, the red-flamed eyes, the big hand holding the gun that was too late.

Kane had guts at that, but he was slow at this front stuff, and Durand, pivoting back, realized swiftly that he should have played Braden first. Braden emerged from behind a tree as Durand pulled around, having moved up as Kane doubled over with one broad hand stitched across his reddening belly.

They met, then, inevitably, and through a smoky haze Durand saw Braden jerk and wilt before his gun with blazing eyes unchanged and fastened upon him. . . .

Walt Durand, the manhunter, stumbled from the nightmare of the jack oaks out into the early sunlight. Two riders hovered here in this strange quiet, then fled. And from down the trail where the hill made its crooked bend among the gray-streaked rocks, a man and a girl raced horses toward him, and, as Durand waited for them, the hardness went out of his eyes.

About the Author

Fred Grove has written extensively in the broad field of Western fiction, from the Civil War and its postwar effect on the expanding West, to modern Quarter horse racing in the Southwest. He has received the Western Writers of America Spur Award five times—for his novels *Comanche Captives* (1961) which also won the Oklahoma Writing Award at the University of Oklahoma and the Levi Strauss Golden Saddleman Award, *The Great Horse Race* (1977), and *Match Race* (1982), and for his short stories, "Comanche Woman" (1963) and "When the *Caballos* Came" (1968). His novel, *The Buffalo Runners* (1968), was chosen for a Western Heritage Award by the National Cowboy Hall of Fame, as was the short story, "Comanche Son" (1961).

He also received a Distinguished Service Award from Western New Mexico University for his regional fiction on the Apache frontier, including the novels *Phantom Warrior* (1981) and *A Far Trumpet* (1985). His recent historical novel, *Bitter Trumpet* (1989), follows the bittersweet adventures of ex-Confederate Jesse Wilder training Juáristas in Mexico fighting the mercenaries of the Emperor Maximilian. *Trail of Rogues* (1993) and *Man on a Red Horse* (1998), *Into the Far Mountains* (1999), and *A Soldier Returns* (2004) are sequels in this frontier saga.

For a number of years Grove worked on newspapers in Oklahoma and Texas as a sportswriter, straight newsman, and editor. Two of his earlier novels, *Warrior Road* (1974) and *Drums Without Warriors* (1976), focus on the brutal Osage murders during the Roaring 'Twenties, a national scandal that brought in the FBI, as does *The Years of Fear*

(Five Star Westerns, 2002). Of Osage descent, the author grew up in Osage County, Oklahoma during the murders. It was while interviewing Oklahoma pioneers that he became interested in Western fiction. He now resides in Tucson, Arizona, with his wife Lucile. His next **Five Star Western** will be *Savage Land*.